God Bless

NEUBRÜCKE

FA SHEPHERD

authorHOUSE®

AuthorHouse™
1663 Liberty Drive
Bloomington, IN 47403
www.authorhouse.com
Phone: 1-800-839-8640

Published by AuthorHouse 06/29/2012

ISBN: 978-1-4772-3197-5 (sc)
ISBN: 978-1-4772-3196-8 (hc)
ISBN: 978-1-4772-3195-1 (e)

Library of Congress Control Number: 2012911619

DISCLAIMER

This book is a work of fiction. The characters and incidents described in the book are products of the author's imagination and are not intended to be construed as real. Any resemblance to actual characters, living or dead, or incidents that may have actually taken place is entirely coincidental. FA Shepherd

This Book is dedicated to the Memory of Jean Ramsey Shepherd

1935 – 2011

She was a Devoted Mother, Grandmother, Wife,
and for more than 57 years, she was also my best friend.

CONTENTS

FOREWORD

Before jumping straightaway headfirst into Neubrücke a quickie history review is in order.

World War II in Europe ended on 8 May 1945 (VE Day) with the capitulation of the German Army. Germanys economic infrastructure had largely collapsed as factories and transportation systems ceased to function. The infrastructure was completely collapsed. The German state had ceased to exist, and sovereign authority passed to the victorious Allied powers. In accordance with the Yalta Conference (aka the Crimea Conference) in February 1945, it was agreed, for purposes of occupation, the Americans, British, French, and Soviets divided Germany into four zones. The American, British, and French zones together made up the western two thirds of Germany, while the Soviet zone comprised the eastern third. Berlin, the former capital, which was surrounded by the Soviet zone, was placed under joint four-power authority but was partitioned into four sectors.

The war in the Pacific ended soon thereafter in August 1945 – celebrated as VJ Day. Concerning the Italian Army war effort: when the first few allied troops set foot on Italian soil in 1943, the entire government collapsed. The Italian Army was never a viable military force for the Axis.

World War II had barely ended in 1945 when China's full-scale civil war resumed in 1946. Four more years of fighting ensued between the

Nationalist China led by Chiang Kai-shek, supported by the United States of America and the Chinese Communist Party led by Mao Zedong, supported by the Union of Soviet Socialist Republics (Russia). 1950 saw the cessation of major military hostilities with the newly founded People's Republic of China controlling mainland China (including Hainan Island, a subdivision region of Guangdong Province at the time until 1988), and the Republic of China's jurisdiction being restricted to Taiwan, Penghu, Quemoy, Matsu and several outlying islands.

Also in 1950, the North Korean communist government's army invaded South Korea. The United Nations condemned the action and military assistance from various member nations were called upon to stop the communist military aggression. A truce was declared in July 1953 which is in existence to this very day. And the storm clouds were brewing in French Indo China with the French and Vietnamese which would eventually result in another war.

After a period of nearly 20 years of continuous hostility, with the loss of multi millions of human lives and the monetary cost of destruction of property impossible to actually determine, why do civilized populations still seem hell bent to bring destruction on each other?

Although the killing machines were rather dormant in the later years of the 1950's, the political agents were being dispatched and the moles had been planted.

Neubrücke: A beautiful, small German village located on the Nahe River in the southwest corner of the Federal Republic of Germany near the border of the Saarland and was within easy driving distance of Belgium, Luxembourg, and France.

Neubrücke had a then population of 416. The population was greatly enhanced by the co-location of the United States Army Hospital Neubrücke. The hospital was manned by personnel of the 98th General

Hospital, the 6th Convalescent Center (at cadre strength) and the 34th Ambulance Train.

Significant Military Installations close by, within 10 miles, were: Baumholder – home of the largest concentration of combat troops in Europe; Hoppstädten – location of an Army airfield and Nike Ajax support units. And just a few "clicks" up the road at Birkenfeld Air Base was stationed an Air Force Air Control Center.

I have known the author of Neubrücke for over 50 years and can attest to the fact that military assignment to the hospital located at Neubrücke was a most memorable experience. Intrigue was on the move, and we were there.

Enjoy the adventure.

CWO *Carl W. Moreland*, US Army, Retired

PREFACE

On November 18, 1957, I arrived at the 6th Convalescence Center in Neubrücke, Germany to complete the remainder of a two year enlistment in the US Army. The 6th CC was part of the US Army's 98th General Hospital Complex. I was a SP5 Personal Specialists and had just been transferred to Germany from Fort Sill, Oklahoma where I had spent the first year of my enlistment. I had volunteered for the active duty assignment out of my Tennessee National Guard Unit in December, 1956 to keep from being drafted. I spent nine miserable days crossing a very stormy North Atlantic Ocean on the USNS Upshur troop ship and most of that time I was hanging over the rail throwing up. It would be the first time I had been away from home on either Thanksgiving or Christmas, and I didn't know anyone in Neubrücke. It had been almost a month since I said goodbye to my wife and got on that Piedmont Air Lines DC 3 at Tri-Cities Airport in East Tennessee for the trip to Fort Dix, New Jersey, and I hadn't seen a familiar face since then. I was one very miserable and homesick GI. I didn't get over that until a couple of sergeants there in the 6th CC barracks asked me to go out with them to experience some of Germany one evening. After about the second or third gasthaus we stopped in that evening I had forgotten all about being homesick.

One of the gasthauses we went to that night was Höhns. Pronounced "Herns" by the GI's. Höhns was in Hoppstädten about two kilometers from the 6th CC. My wife Jean and I lived there for four months during the summer of 1958 in one room upstairs over the bar area when she later came to Germany to be with me. I would sometimes bring Carl and Louis, those two sergeants that helped me get over my homesickness, home with me for supper. Jean never knew how many she was going to have to feed in that little room. Carl became my best friend, and after almost 55 years we still remain in touch. I can't begin to imagine what my year in Neubrücke might have been like if it hadn't been for him. Before Jean came over, Carl and I spent many happy hours in Höhns and all the other gasthauses in the area including one truly unforgettable night at Höhns during the German Fasching Celebration.

There were three other young army couples living at Höhns and the eight of us would get together two or three times a week. Either downstairs in the bar area or in one of our rooms. We were all in the same circumstance and spending time together made it seem like having family there. Shortly before Jean had to come home because of some serious health problems her mother was having we had moved to The Four Daughters Gasthaus in Neubrücke. We had a two room suite there, but only lived in it about a month before Jean had to come home and I moved back into the barracks.

As I was clearing post before leaving Fort Sill my old boss told me I was being given the opportunity of a lifetime. I was being handed a ten thousand dollar paid vacation he said. On the trip over when I was puking my guts out and during those first few miserable homesick days it sure didn't seem much like a vacation. However, after Carl and Louis took me out to the gasthauses that night and Jean later came over to be with me, that's just what it turned out to be. We got to see things and visit places that most folks only get to dream about.

On July 17, 1958, our fourth wedding anniversary; we had breakfast in Sargans, Switzerland, lunch in Innsbruck, Austria, and dinner in Garmisch, Germany. Then, after spending the night in a restored SS barracks which was now the army's General Walker R&R Hotel in

Berchtesgaden, Germany, we spent the next day on top of a mountain exploring Hitler's Kehlsteinhause. We later spent a wonderful weekend sightseeing in Luxembourg, and were making plans to spend a few days at the World's Fair in Brussels, Belgium when Jean received the news about her mom's health problems. It had indeed been just what that old Chief Warrant Officer at Fort Sill had told me it would be.

So far as I know there were no spies or secret agents at the 98th Hospital while I was there. However, it is the memories from my year with the 6th CC in Neubrücke, Germany in 1958 that was the inspiration for this work of fiction about spies and secret agents.

FA Shepherd

98th General Hospital, Neubrücke, Germany.

SP5 FA Shepherd at work in the 98th Hospital's
message center in Neubrücke, Germany, 1958.

PROLOGUE

In July, 1945, barely two months after the German surrender, Harry Truman, Winston Churchill and Joseph Stalin met in Potsdam, Germany to decide the fate of post war Germany. Most historians trace the beginnings of the Cold War to this historic conference. The partitioning of Germany after the war had in principle already been agreed to at a similar conference in Yalta several months before the meeting in Potsdam. Franklin Roosevelt was the American president at that conference and some said he had sold out the western allies to appease the Russians. At Potsdam, Truman simply agreed to the previous commitments made by Roosevelt.

The western allies basically disagreed on how the European map should look after the war. Churchill in particular didn't want the Russians to have as much control and power. He had totally disagreed with the way Germany had been partitioned, and in a speech given in Fulton, Missouri in 1946, he proclaimed that an Iron Curtain had descended across Eastern Europe. Reaching from Stettin in the Baltic to Trieste in the Adriatic.

The partitioning plan the allies had finally settled on divided Germany into four zones of occupation and influence. The Russian zone would be all of Germany east of the Elbe River, including the city of Berlin. The rest of Germany would be divided between the British zone to the north, the US zone to the south, and a small French zone in the southwest. The city of Berlin would also be divided into four zones. Almost as soon as the boundaries had been drawn the Russians closed off their zone, including in Berlin, to the rest of the world.

The seeds of deceit and espionage had been sown long before the end of the war. Stalin became highly suspicious and believed the British and Americans had conspired to ensure the Soviets bore the brunt of the fighting against Nazi Germany. According to his view, the western allies had deliberately delayed opening a second front in order to step in at the last moment and shape the peace settlement. Thus, the Soviets perception of the west left a strong undercurrent of tension and hostility between the allied powers. It didn't help the situation any when President Truman told Stalin about the atomic bomb while they were in Potsdam. One week after the Potsdam Conference a lone B29 Super Fortress dropped the bomb on Hiroshima, ushering in the atomic age.

Spies and spying became a part of the Cold War game. Both sides used spies as a way of acquiring knowledge of what the other side was doing, or to spread false knowledge about what was going on. Spies could become double agents, and the whole spy story has developed a rather romantic image as a result of western film portrayals of spies. However, for all of them, spying was far from romantic – it was a highly dangerous job, and many worked knowing there was barely any chance of being rescued if caught. Both sides involved in the Cold War used spies from all walks of life and backgrounds. The ability to seamlessly blend into the background was vital. Many spies with this capability had soon been assimilated into all walks of Russian and American life. The bulk of them with some sort of diplomatic status.

The extent to which the establishment had been infiltrated will probably never be known. However, Joseph McCarthy, a little known senator from Wisconsin put it all in perspective in 1950 when he asserted in a speech that large numbers of Communist spies had infiltrated the American State Department, including the US Army. His accusations led to what became known as the McCarthy Communist Witch Hunt during the Korean War.

His accusations, although never substantiated, fueled widespread fears of Communist infiltration in America. Sometimes turning neighbor against neighbor, and friend against friend. Hollywood was turned upside down by these accusations that caused rivalries and hatreds among the actors and producers that still exist today.

When the Soviet Union shocked the world with the surprise launching of their Sputnik Satellite on October 4, 1957 it was a huge blow to American pride and caught the Space Agency as well as American intelligence agencies with their pants down. When a series of meaningless documents about a remote army hospital started showing up in the hands of the East German secret police, American intelligence agencies became alarmed that it was about to happen again. US agents were sent to the region to learn what was going on, and a new game of they spy – we spy began. While stationed at this backwater outpost in occupied Germany during the height of the cold war, these US agents soon discover a Communists plot to steal the secrets of a new computer communications technology that would give the Soviets an even greater advantage in the space race.

Residents in the sleepy little village of Neubrücke, Germany and the military personnel stationed there with the recently deployed 98th General Hospital are blissfully unaware of the spy games going on around them. In this remote outpost in the French Zone of occupation in the southwest corner of Germany, the beer is good, the duty is mostly boring, and the only problem the GI's stationed there have is trying to decide which gasthaus they will be going to tonight. However, when the 7424th Support Squadron starts remodeling and restructuring the Air Force communication facilities at the nearby Birkenfeld Tactical Air Base their world is about to be changed forever. Almost as soon as construction starts, rumors start spreading that what was advertised as just an upgrade to the existing facilities is in reality the installation of a top secret communications facility. As a result, Russian KGB and East German Stasi agents are sent to investigate. When Washington responds by sending in agents of their own, Neubrücke, and the American GI's stationed there are about to enter the Cold War.

ONE

THE CID AGENTS

A cold black rain mixed with snow was falling that December afternoon when the sergeant walked into the 6th Convalescence Center Orderly Room in Neubrücke, Germany and set down his duffle bag. SP4 Hale, the company clerk, started to get up and help him just as First Sergeant Charlie Smith came through the other door.

"I'm Sergeant Stevens reporting for duty," the new arrival said.

"Who," -- and before Sergeant Smith could finish his question Stevens was on the floor.

"Somebody get some help!" Smith yelled as he got on the floor beside Stevens and started trying to revive him. It was only a matter of minutes before first responder medics from the 98th General Hospital were on the scene giving Stevens the aid he needed. After they revived and stabilized him they rushed him to the hospital's emergency room. After extensive testing, the ER doctors determined that Sergeant Stevens had been poisoned and had him admitted to one of the hospital's Intensive Care Units.

"Who was that?" Smith asked Hale when he came back from the ICU.

"I don't know, but I did find these papers he was carrying. It looks like he was being assigned here."

"Were we expecting any new men?"

"Not that I know of, but these orders are from 7th Army headquarters," Hale said as he handed the papers to Smith. Sergeant Smith took the papers and walked slowly over to his desk, reading the orders as he went. Sergeant First Class William Stevens is hereby relieved of duty 7th Army Headquarters Stuttgart, Germany pending reassignment. Sergeant

1

Stevens will report to the commanding officer 6th Convalescence Center, Neubrücke, Germany no later than seventeen hundred hours, 6 December, 1957. Benjamin Johnson, General, Commanding.

Next morning Sergeant Smith was just starting on his second cup of coffee when a major with a 7th army patch on his left shoulder walked into his orderly room. "AT EASE!" Hale yelled, startling Smith, and causing him to spit a mouthful of coffee on the copy of Stars and Stripes he was reading. Looking up to see what was going on Smith recognized the major and asked, "What the hell is the CID doing here?"

"And a good morning to you too," the newcomer said, "It's been a long time Charlie."

"Not nearly long enough," Sergeant Smith replied.

"Let's go in Captain Worley's office and I will explain to you both what the CID is doing here," the Major said.

Sergeant Smith got up and walked over to his CO's office door and knocked. When he heard an "Enter!" from the other side of the door, he opened it and ushered the major into the office.

"Good morning Captain," Sergeant Smith said as they went through the door. "This is Major Johnny Bradley from the CID, and he would like a word with you."

As Captain Worley started to get up, Johnny told him to keep his seat and motioned for Sergeant Smith to be seated as well. The Major walked over to the window and while looking out at the snow covered grass between the two buildings he said, "Yesterday a Sergeant Stevens reported here for duty, but as soon as he reported in he became ill and passed out."

Before he could continue Sergeant Smith asked, "How did you find out about that so fast?"

The Major turned around, and while walking back to the center of the office said, "I have my sources."

"Yeah, I had forgotten how well informed you are."

"Now if I may continue," Johnny said. "It is really First Lieutenant

Stevens, and he is a CID special investigator. He was to be here on a special under cover assignment."

"What's going on?" Captain Worley asked.

"We believe there is a Commie spy ring operating in this area, and may very well be operating right here out of the 98th Hospital," Johnny said. "We have been monitoring a lot of reports of suspicious activity but haven't been able to put a name or face on any of it yet. The Russian units in East Germany not only know how many troops are stationed here, but they know how many patients are in the hospital on any given day and even what the mess hall is serving for supper. How do we know that? We know just as much about what is going on in their units. They spy on us and we spy on them. It's the game we play. However, when the shooting starts it won't be a game any longer. That's why we need to find out who these people are and put them out of business. We've had an agent here for some time now, but he hasn't been able to get the job done. Lt. Stevens was being assigned here to give him some help. A replacement agent is already on his way here. However, since Stevens was taken out like he was we think there may be a leak somewhere in our chain of command so only two folks know about his replacement. The commanding general of 7th Army and myself. When or how he arrives is being kept a close secret. We also think Lt. Stevens may have seen or heard something either before he left to come down here or on his way here, and that is why he was taken out. Because of that he is still in danger and will be moved to a much safer location as soon as he is well enough to be moved. Until then, he will be under twenty four hour armed guard, and they have orders to shoot to kill."

"If you don't know who these people are how do you know one of the guards is not one of them?" Smith asked.

"They weren't picked at random. Contrary to what some of you may think we are not stupid."

"You keep saying Lt. Stevens was taken out, what do you mean?" Worley asked.

"His problem didn't result from natural causes, and that's all I am able to tell you about that. Also, I will remain in the area and be in charge of this operation. The new man will take orders only from me and report directly to me. He will of course be in your command and will observe all military courtesy towards you while he is here. After he arrives he will be assigned to the 98th Hospital's message center. Are there any questions?"

"I have lots of questions," Smith said. "But, none that you would answer. Are the men guarding Lt. Stevens in any danger?"

"That will be up to them," the Major said. "They have their orders and whether they choose to get hurt or shoot will be their choice. Personally I hope they are brave enough to shoot and are excellent marksmen. Bill is a friend of mine."

The 6th Convalescence Center is located at the 98th General Hospital Complex and it is the only active convalescence hospital in the army. It is designated as the United States Army in Europe or USAREUR Convalescent Center. At full strength it could operate a fifteen hundred bed hospital but is now operating at about cadre strength, and in the process of being deactivated. Out of the thirty men now in the company only ten of them actually work for the 6th CC and only about half of these are medical or physical therapy related positions. The rest of the men now in the unit are working in various positions in the 98th Hospital. Most of these are noncoms in charge of the sections in which they are assigned. Something that is not too well received by the 98th personnel.

Neubrücke, Germany is a small village of about two hundred located on the Nahe River in Birkenfeld County in the extreme southwestern section of Germany near the Saar border. It is primarily a farming section, and before the hospital complex that provided most of them with jobs was built, it was home to one of the poorest populations in Germany. Neubrücke is in the western area command of Europe and is in the French Zone. Most of the troops in WACOM are assigned to COMZ. All American troops in Germany at this time are either in or under the command of the 7th Army.

The 98th General Hospital was activated in 1943 at Fort Jackson, South Carolina. It served in England during the war and in various locations in Germany after the war, including Munich where it was located before the move to Neubrücke. The buildings for the hospitals present location were constructed on a small hill just above the Neubrücke Bahnhof in 1954. Soon after construction was begun the army engineers discovered the hill site that had been selected for the hospital's location was in reality the site of a Celtic burial ground. The site called a 'Tumuli' consisted of twelve large earthen mounds that had to be excavated before construction could continue. The relics and bones that were found are on display at the Landesmuseum in Trier. After removal of all relics, construction was resumed and the fifty five building hospital complex was completed.

In its present configuration it is more a collection of specialty clinics than general hospital. It operates a thousand bed hospital with approximately four hundred enlisted men and two hundred officers. Most of the officers are doctors and nurses. Some of the specialty clinics are an EENT clinic, the rehab center, an orthopedic clinic and a chest center and one of the best equipped and staffed emergency rooms in Europe. The 98th is the orthopedic center of USAREUR and when the deactivation of the 6th CC is completed the 98th will also become the rehab center for all of USAREUR. The hospital complex is located between the little village of Neubrücke and the Saar border which is about one kilometer to the west. One of the largest garrisons of troops in Western Germany is located in Baumholder about ten kilometers away.

Also, located at the hospital is the 34th Ambulance Train. These personnel staff and operate the only military medical transportation and evacuation train in the American zone. It is a fully equipped medical facility and can, if required, operate totally independent of any outside assistance for up to ten days. The hospital train usually makes a trip at least once a month to Frankfurt's Rhine Maine Air Base transporting patients that are being evacuated back to the states. During this trip it makes a stop at the 97th

Hospital in Landstuhl to pick up any patients that are being evacuated from there. The 34th Ambulance Train is the only ambulance train still on active status in the US Army. Most medical emergencies and evacuations are now being made as needed by helicopter. In the event of war, the train would be used to evacuate as many patients as possible to the hospital's fallback position on the coast of France.

"Let me see if I understand this?" Worley said. "There's almost a thousand army personnel, both men and women stationed here and about half that many more German civilians employed by the army working here. They are being used in positions anywhere from secretaries in the most sensitive positions to cooks, to mechanics, to pushfraus. Not to mention all the Red Cross employees and Special Services people that are here. Any one of almost fifteen hundred individuals, both German and American, could be your spy and you thought only one man was going to get the job done? You are either the most optimistic SOB I ever saw, or the biggest fool." Sergeant Smith laughed in spite of all efforts to keep from it.

"You're enjoying this aren't you," Bradley said.

"I was in Korea when the CID got involved in that Joe McCarthy Communist witch hunt foolishness," Worley said. "Are you planning to turn this into another mess like that?"

"We were just following orders back then, and that's what we plan to do this time."

"As I recall some of your people had a very peculiar way of interpreting their orders."

"I wouldn't know about that, I wasn't there."

"Maybe not, but you were in Oklahoma a couple of years ago weren't you," Smith said. "Were you just carrying out orders then?" Bradley gave him a dirty look and got up to leave.

When they came out of Captain Worley's office Sergeant Smith said, "Men this is Major Bradley with the army CID. He's going to be in the area for a while, and as long as he is here anything you see or hear in this office stays in the office. Any breach of this directive will result in severe punishment. Corporal Jones, effective immediately you are relieved of all duties with the 6th CC and will be providing the Major with any assistance he may require, including transportation and acting as his guide. Do you have anything to add Major?"

"No," He said, and when he turned to leave Smith followed him out the door.

"What's going on?" Jones asked Hale.

"I don't know. What would the CID be interested in here?"

"Maybe it has something to do with what happened yesterday," Jones said. "Whatever it is Smith didn't seem too happy to see that major. Did you hear what they said to each other when he came in? Sergeant Smith knew him from somewhere before."

"Life around here may be about to get interesting," Hale said. "I'd give a months' pay to hear what's going on outside right now."

"What are you trying to pull?" Smith asked the major when they got outside.

"I'm not trying to pull anything," the major said. "I'm just trying to do my job."

"If just doing your job causes a mess here like the one you made in Oklahoma it will be the last job you ever have."

"Don't threaten me Sergeant."

"That wasn't a threat Major, it was a promise. I won't just sit and watch while you make some other GI's life miserable like you did mine. You mess with any of my men and I'll take you down. I've got my twenty years in and seeing you fall would be the best way I could think of to end my career."

"Fuck you Sergeant," And, the major got in his jeep and drove off.

After his confrontation with Smith the major went looking for Claude. Sergeant Claude Morelocke was the hospital supply sergeant. He was also a CID agent, but was having to learn by on the job training what he was supposed to be doing. His boss, Major Bradley, had been very little help with that, and seemed to be more interested in keeping an eye on him than teaching him his job. He wasn't at all surprised when the major walked into his supply room this morning. He knew that Lt. Stevens had been sent in, and what had happened to him. He had been told that Stevens was being sent in to help him, but knew it was just another of Bradleys way of keeping an eye on him.

"How's Bill?" he asked when Bradley walked in.

"He's going to be OK. It was poison, but we don't yet know what kind or how or when. As soon as they say he can be moved he will be taken to Landstuhl. We're going to let it leak that he died. Any idea who's behind this Claude?"

"If I had to arrest someone right now it would be Hans Müller."

"Who's Hans Müller?"

"He owns the Four Daughters Gasthaus just outside the front gate here and is a Nazi through and through. He hates Americans and will do anything he can to harm us. He was a Tiger Tank Commander in one of their Panzer units and as far as he's concerned the war is still going on. You sending someone down here to take Bills place?"

"Frank Shipley is on his way as we speak. Do you know him?"

"Yeah, we've shared a few beers together. He's a good man."

"Bring him up to speed and show him around when he gets here. He'll be working in the message center. I'm going to hang around for a while, but you are not to know me if we happen to cross paths."

"Yes Sir," Claude said and he gave him a mock salute as the major walked out the door. Before Bradley got to the car he turned and said, "What did you do to get the MP's so pissed off at you?"

"Oh it's nothing, just a little misunderstanding about some crystals for their radios."

After coming back inside when Major Bradley left, Sergeant Smith went back in Captain Worley's office.

"Something's not right about all this Captain," he said.

"I get that feeling too," the captain said. "For starters, the CID doesn't have any agents in East Germany like he indicated. Hell, I don't even think they usually get involved in spy hunts. I also think he was lying about Korea. If I'm not mistaken I remember him from somewhere, and I think it was Korea. What was that business about Oklahoma?"

"We were both in one of the artillery units there at Fort Sill a couple of years ago just before I was transferred over here. It wasn't pretty. He was working some kind of case there that almost resulted in my being court martialed. The man is bad news Captain."

"Keep an eye on him. Let him do his job, and if he gets out of line let me know. If he does get out of line or cause any trouble, I'll sic Colonel Hodge on him. That ought to take some of the starch out of his khakis." Smith left the office laughing, and when he came out Hale was waiting for him.

"OK Sergeant, what is going on?" he asked.

"What do you mean?"

"You know damned well what I am talking about. I saw and heard the conversation between you two when he came in here. Where do you know him from?"

"Our paths crossed back in the states. I had just become the First Sergeant of one of the artillery companies at Fort Sill. There had been some problems in the unit before I was assigned there. Major Bradley was sent in to investigate. Either he hadn't been given all the details or he for some reason decided I was the guilty party. Anyway he almost ruined my military career."

"Sounds interesting. What was it you did?"

"I hadn't done anything. It had all happened before I got there. However, Major Bradley didn't believe that. He showed up there one day pretty much like Sgt. Stevens did here. PFC Bradley came in unexpected with orders assigning him to our battalion. He was assigned as my company clerk. I had no way of knowing who or what he was and didn't find out until the court martial that he was a CID Major."

"Who's court martial?"

"Mine. That's why I assigned Jones to him. I expect him to keep me informed about Major Bradleys every move while he is here." Smith wasn't about to tell Hale, about the other CID agent that Bradley had said was already at the hospital. Wonder who he is Smith said to himself. He didn't think anyone in his orderly room was CID, but he would be extra careful of anything he said or did just in case. He knew firsthand how Bradley operated.

While they were talking a medevac helicopter was landing in front of hospital headquarters. As soon as the rotors slowed two corpsmen who had been waiting at the front of the hospital pushed a gurney up to the open door of the helicopter and helped the lone corpsman in the helicopter slide a litter containing a sheet covered body onto the gurney. They then moved the gurney through the hospital doors that were being held open by the hospital Sergeant Major. As they rolled the gurney down the hall they were passed by another gurney on its way to the waiting helicopter. As Lt. Stevens was being loaded into the helicopter, SP5 Frank Shipley was rolling off the other gurney in the hospital ER. By the time the helicopter carrying Lt. Stevens had lifted off from the hospital, SP5 Shipley was reporting in to First Sergeant Charlie Smith. All the orders he handed to Smith said was that he was being reassigned to the 6th CC from 7th Army Headquarters. However, Smith couldn't help but notice the orders were exactly like the ones he had looked at the day before. Only the name had been changed. He didn't want the rest of his orderly room staff to know what was going on and didn't say anything. However, as he was escorting Shipley into Captain Worley's office he quietly asked him if Bradley had sent him.

"Yes, but I'd appreciate it if no one else knew."

"Don't worry, no one will know about it from me."

Several nights later Sergeant Smith was sitting in Höhn's Gasthaus enjoying a beer when the major walked in.

"Mind if I join you?" He said as he pulled up a chair and sat down.

"As a matter of fact I do," Smith said.

"How long are you going to go around with that chip on your shoulder Charlie?"

"As long as you are in the area."

"Look, Johnny said, it's time we cleared the air."

"There's nothing to clear. You are an arrogant horses ass and while I may have to work with you I don't have to respect you or share my free time with you," and he started to get up and leave.

"Please sit back down and hear me out."

"Why should I? You damn near ruined my career by having me court martialed. If that general hadn't agreed to review my case I would be somewhere in Oklahoma now, working on an oil rig."

"Who do you think gave that general all he needed to review your case and have all the charges dismissed?"

"What?" Charlie said as he sat back down.

"That's right. I did have you court martialed, but your precious military career was never in any danger. I had to get you out of the way so the real crooks would think they had gotten away with it. I knew all along you were innocent and so did the general."

"How many other people around here know about what happened back there at Fort Sill?"

"None of that ever got put in your records. The only thing to come out of that as far as you are concerned is that you were sent over here to finish out your career instead of ending your time in the army at Fort Sill. I know we've had our differences in the past, but putting a stop to what's going on around here now is much more important than what you may think about me. I need your help and cooperation."

"What can I do?"

"Right now I need for you to give SP5 Shipley permission to live off post."

"He has to be married before I can do that."

"No, he has to be married before you can pay him an extra allowance for living on the economy. I need for him to live at The Four Daughters for a while. I want him to keep an eye on Hans Müller."

Hans had named his gasthaus The Four Daughters in honor of his four girls and all of them worked at various jobs there. But mostly as bar hops. Hans was very proud of his girls but had become increasingly upset by their continued flirting with the American service men. It seemed the more he warned them about their flirting the more they enjoyed the flirting. The Four Daughters was one of the most popular gasthauses at the hospital because it was just outside the front gate and the GI's could walk there. Walking was the only means of transportation most of them had. The girls had learned long ago that flirting with the GI's would get them better tips, and they had become expert at it. Hans didn't approve of this and had on more than one occasion threatened them and the GI's for doing it.

The Four Daughters is in a three story building and one of the largest gasthauses in the area. The top two floors contain rental rooms, and most of them are permanently rented to GI couples. The closest army housing is in Baumholder over ten kilometers away, and all of the army housing over there is for noncoms and officers. Any GI below the rank of E5 with a family in this area of Germany has to live on the economy and this usually means living in a gasthaus, at least for a while. Hans Müller is more than happy to sell the GI's beer and rent rooms to them, but that is as far as his association with Americans goes. He hates their guts and doesn't hesitate to let anyone who will listen know it. He particularly doesn't want his girls having anything to do with the Americans. SP 5 Shipley rented a room on the second floor just above the front entrance to the gasthaus and began watching Hans. However, most of his time there was spent watching Hans' four girls.

Frank hadn't seen Claude since completing advanced military police training at Fort Gordon, Georgia more than a year ago. Sergeant Morelocke had been one of his instructors there. Frank had been assigned to the Provost Marshal's office at Fort Sill, Oklahoma after his MP training. Tracking down the occasional theft or bogus check report wasn't the duty Frank had in mind when he applied for CID school. The weekend trips into the nearby Wichita Mountains for a picnic or cook out were pleasant diversions, but he wanted more action. He welcomed the reassignment to

Neubrücke, Germany, even if he had no idea where it was. As soon as he was settled in at the gasthaus his first job would be to find Claude.

Claude Morelocke had grown up on the family farm in Ohio. He led his high school football team to a state championship and was planning to attend Ohio State on a football scholarship. However, the Korean War changed those plans when he was drafted into the army just two months after graduation. After basic and advanced infantry training at Fort Riley, Kansas he was assigned as a rifleman replacement to the 1st Cavalry Division, 8th Cavalry Regiment, 1st Battalion, Charlie Company just before they were scheduled to take part in the amphibious landings at Inchon. The 8th Calvs participation in those landings was canceled, and the regiment instead landed on the southeastern coast of Korea at Pohang-dong eighty miles north of Pusan. The North Koreans were twenty five miles away when elements of the 1st Cavalry Division went ashore in the first amphibious landing of the Korean War. The 8th Cav, reinforced by division artillery and other units, moved by rail, truck and jeep to relieve the 21st Regiment of the 24th Division near Yongdong.

The regiment successfully continued their northward push and was deep into North Korea just south of the Yalu River near Unsan when the Communist Chinese entered the war. On November 1, 1950, the Chinese attacked the 8th Cav all along its line. Thousands of Communist Chinese Forces attacked and soon the 8th Cav was surrounded. They fell back in total disarray into the city of Unsan, and the men took to the hills. Only a few scattered survivors made it back to tell their story. In essence, the 8th Calvary Regiment ceased to exist as a fighting unit on that day. PFC Morelocke, just six months out of high school was one of the survivors. But his fight wasn't over. After he had made his way back to the American lines, he was assigned to the 3rd Battalion and fought with them for the rest of the war. On December 30, 1951, after five hundred and forty nine days of continuous fighting, Morelocke and the rest of the 1st Cavalry Division was sent back to Hokkaido, Japan. When the truce was finally declared the POW survivors from the 8th Cav that had been taken captive at Unsan walked back across the thirty eighth Parallel to rejoin their buddies. The First Team had performed tough duties with honor, pride and valor. Morelocke was proud of his service with the 8th Cav, but wanted nothing more to do with the army. All he wanted now was to be sent home and discharged.

Claude returned to Ohio and tried to pick up his life. However, he soon learned it would never again be the same for him. He had only been home for a couple of months when the nightmares started. Each one would be slightly different, but would all end almost the same way, with him trying to claw his way out of that barn. When he finally left home again several months later there were scars on the headboard of his bed made while he was trying to claw his way out of that barn during his dreams. Three of the men had decided to stick together when they literally crawled out of Unsan that night. After leaving the town they had taken refuge in a cave the next day. One of them kept watch while the others slept. As it turned out, that days rest would be the only one they got for the next week. They had planned to move around only at night, but with the Chinese soldiers all around them they sometimes had to keep moving during the day to keep from being discovered. The Chinese knew the 8th Cav men had bugged out into the hills and were always on the lookout for any of the survivors. The three men had vowed not to be taken captive and kept moving as much as they could to the south. A few days before they reached freedom the men had hidden themselves in a small barn. The sentry woke the others up when he saw some soldiers approaching the barn. They barely made their way out the back of the barn just as the Chinese soldiers came in the front. Two nights later they passed through the Chinese lines and were reunited with some soldiers from the 24th Division.

In Claude's dreams, he would sometimes be on a mountain top watching the battle going on below him. Other times he would be in a village going from house to house throwing grenades and shooting the Chinese as they tried to escape. Sometimes, he would be alone, and other times he would be with his buddies. The most recurring theme in his dream had him being ambushed while leading a patrol. They had stopped in an orchard and were enjoying their C Rations when all of a sudden the air was filled with some of the most hideous bugle music he had ever heard, and the Chinese soldiers came screaming out of the woods all around them. Everyone had been killed but him and just as they were about to bayonet him, he would be back in that barn trying to claw his way out. No matter how the dreams started, or what he was doing in them, they always ended with him in that barn trying to escape as the Chinese came for him. He tried drinking as an escape, but found the only thing that did was cause hangovers. The doctors told him that only time would bring relief.

After bouncing around from one odd job to the next for a little more than a year he went to the recruiting office and told them he would reenlist if they would take him back in as a sergeant. They agreed, and he was sent to Fort Gordon, Georgia as an instructor in the advanced MP school. Because of his background and experience during the Korean War Sergeant Morelocke became an escape and evasion instructor. He not only instructed his students how to remain alive while trapped behind enemy lines, but how to cause as much confusion and destruction as possible while getting safely back to their own forces. Claude didn't realize until he had been sent to Germany to look for spies that he had somehow become a CID agent.

When he arrived at the 6th Convalescent Center in Neubrücke, Germany he wondered what he had done to deserve this. He knew nothing about being a counterspy, but he knew enough to know that someone would have to be crazy to think there were spies in this place. However, if he had learned anything from his experience in Korea it was to become as inconspicuous as possible, and that was what he intended to do now. Becoming the hospital's supply sergeant gave him the opportunity he needed to blend quietly into the background. He had been in Germany for almost a year when Frank arrived.

When Frank walked into the supply warehouse that afternoon the only person he saw had his back to the door. "Sergeant Morelocke?" he asked.

The sergeant turned around to see who was speaking to him and immediately recognized Frank.

"Frank Shipley," he said.

"I wasn't sure you would remember me."

"Sure I do. We had some good ole times back there at Gordon. That was a memorable graduation shindig we had with your group. How have you been?"

"Bored to death is how I've been. Tracking down petty crooks was not what you trained me for."

"Are you settled in? I haven't seen you around the barracks."

"I'm not in the barracks. Bradley wanted me to stay at The Four Daughters Gasthaus so I could keep an eye on the owner, a Hans Müller."

"That's probably my fault," Claude said. "When Stevens was poisoned, Bradley asked me who could have done it, and I told him the first place I'd look would be at The Four Daughters, and Hans. Sorry about that."

"Don't be. The scenery there is probably a lot better than looking a bunch of hairy legged men in the barracks. What's Hans all about anyway?"

"Hans is still a Nazi fighting WW II. He was a Tiger Tank commander in one of Colonel Hess' Panzer Battalions at Bastogne. He was with Hess in Russia before that. He's willing to take our money selling beer and renting rooms to us, but don't turn you back on him or try to mess around with one of his girls."

"Is he one of the spies?"

"No, just a sore loser."

"What have you found out about spies around here?"

"Not a whole lot. What did they tell you?"

"Nothing. Just there had been reports of spying around here, and that I would be working with you to try and learn what was going on."

"Two, maybe three weeks after that Sputnik thing went up one of the CIA operatives in East Germany intercepted a report about this hospital,"

Claude said. "After locating this place and seeing what it was they wondered why, and thought it had to be a new code and turned it over to their code boys. While they were still trying to figure that one out a second message was intercepted. The agency panicked. After getting caught with their pants down when that Sputnik thing went up they weren't about to let that happen again, so they sent one of their own over here to investigate. Somewhere along the line the pentagon found out about it and said this was an army post, and as such the investigation should be done by the CID. I don't know why I drew the short straw, but I was the one they sent over here. Anyway, before I had a chance to get my feet on the ground Bradley showed up and wanted Stevens brought in to keep an eye on me, and you know the rest of the story."

"I was told there might be a spy ring here," Frank said.

"That's what Bradley has been saying. He's been trying to convince Washington and the 7th Army there is a gang or spy ring here."

"You don't sound convinced."

"Look around you. What in the world would be around here that it would take a gang or ring to look for? The answer they are looking for should not be who, but why."

"What do you know about Bradley?"

"Nothing much, but if first impressions count, I don't like nor trust the man," Claude said. "Did you know him before this?"

"I knew of him, or about him. But no, I didn't know him," Frank said. "He had been involved in some sort of scandal just before I got to Fort Sill. The story was that someone was stealing and selling weapons, and apparently Bradley had been sent in to investigate. He came in as a PFC and was assigned as a clerk in one of the artillery companies. Neither the Provost Marshal nor the base commander had been informed that Bradley was there. The Provost Marshal had been investigating the gun running rumors and was about to make an arrest when all hell broke loose. Bradley had come to the conclusion that one of the artillery company first sergeants was the guilty party and had him arrested and was planning to have him court martialed. That's the first time that Colonel Longbow, who was the Provost Marshal, knew the CID was involved and he was livid. Longbow is a full bloodied Comanche Indian and believe me I know from personal experience you don't want him mad at you. Longbow knew the first sergeant was innocent and went to the base commander with the evidence. The general had all the charges dropped and Bradley then brought charges up against Longbow for interfering with his case. The three men continued to fight over who was guilty of what, who had jurisdiction when they finally did decide if someone was guilty, and who actually had the authority to do anything. The general finally had enough and told both Bradley and Longbow that he was the one with the stars and that gave him the authority. He ordered Bradley off the base and told Longbow to continue with his investigation. However, while all that was going on the company commander of one of the artillery companies caught one of his platoon leaders in bed with his wife and had the lieutenant shipped out to Korea. It just so happened, the lieutenant was the one Longbow had been investigating. You talk about one pissed off Provost Marshal. They said he had to be restrained to keep him from killing Bradley. I arrived there shortly after that. Longbow didn't want anything to do with any more CID cops, so I wound up being mostly a clerk. I made friends with the post Sergeant Major and told him to find me the first transfer out of there, and here I am. I had no idea where or what a Neubrücke was. But, I was more disappointed to find out that I would be working for Bradley than I was to see what this place is."

"That ties in with some of the rumors I've been hearing about him," Claude said. "But don't sell this place short. It may look like the end of the world to you now, however it does have its advantages. The beer here is good and the duty couldn't be any better. The remoteness of this place keeps the army from sticking its nose into what goes on around here. This place sort of grows on you. I've come to like it here and I think in time you will too."

"Now for the sixty four dollar question," Frank said. "Why is the CID getting involved in looking for Spies?"

"Your guess is as good as mine. However, I do have a theory. I think word got out the CIA was looking for spies here and Bradley thought he should be involved. I think he sees this as a way to pick up some brownie points and maybe get himself promoted."

"Will he be that actively involved?"

"No. What he will do is sit back and let us do all the work, then step in and take all the credit for it when we catch the bad guys."

"How do you figure that?"

"Just a gut feeling. I don't trust him. Did you receive any special training in looking for spies?"

"No!"

"Neither did I. I think we are being used."

"We might as well play along and enjoy it, don't you think? Bradley told me to show you around, so how about I pick you up this evening and show you some of the sights around here?" Claude asked. "I'll show you a couple of the other gasthauses in the area and introduce you to some good German beer. I think you'll find it's much better than that 3.2 stuff we had to put up with at the PX in Gordon."

"Sounds like fun," Frank said.

When Claude arrived at The Four Daughters that evening Frank was out front waiting for him. "First stop, Gasthaus Höhn," Claude said as Frank was getting in the car. When they walked into Höhns the juke box was playing the most popular song in Germany at the time. Fraulein by Bobby Helms. Frank knew they had come to the right place. After drinking about half of his bottle of beer Frank said, "You were right. This is a lot better than that PX stuff, and the music here is a lot better also. The view ain't bad either."

"Keep your wee-wee in your pants Hoss," Claude said. "All those gals you are looking at are army wives. Some of them live upstairs here with their husbands. Like most rural gasthauses in Germany, this is a Mom and Pop small business and family kind of place. A lot of the gasthauses around here have been in the same family for generations. Next to The Four Daughters this is the most popular gasthaus at the hospital."

"I can understand why," Frank said.

"These places will probably be a good source of information while we look for spies," Claude said. "If it happens at or around the hospital, sooner or later someone in here will be talking about it. All we have to do is keep our eyes and ears open."

"What's with the EM Club?" Frank asked. "I was almost forced to buy a club card. Well maybe not forced, but I was sure made to feel like I needed one."

"Yeah, that's Smith's doing. The club manager is one of the only other master sergeants in the outfit and a buddy of Smiths. Every payday he will be sitting next to Smith, and as soon as you get your pay he will have his hand out with a club card with your name on it. You do feel like you are being forced to buy one. It's a good investment though. Nickel beer every Friday night, and a good place to kill an evening. They do have some decent entertainment coming in all the time. Good country bands and other stuff at least once a month, and the only price of admission is your club card. That will also probably be an excellent place to pick up some good gossip. You about ready to go? I want to show you one other place tonight."

"Where are we going now?" Frank asked as they were backing out of the parking lot at Höhns.

"To a place over near Dienstweiler called The Edelweiss."

The Edelweiss Gasthaus was back off the road in a little grove of trees. It was in an old house. Unlike most of the newer gasthauses, this one didn't have one large room with a bar, but the rooms of the old house had been turned into seating areas. Some of the doors had been widened to give the appearance of a larger area. It was very unique and homey.

"To really appreciate it you need to see it in the daylight," Claude said. "It's an old farm house and must have been really something in its day." After they had been seated, Frank said he needed a bathroom. Claude showed him where it was and went back to their table. Frank returned in a minute looking like he had seen a ghost.

"There's a woman in there," he said. Claude couldn't hold it in any longer and let out a hefty laugh.

"You knew all along!" Frank said.

"She's what we call a Latrine Frau," Claude said. "She's not in there to look at you. The only interest she has in you is how much of a tip are you going to leave."

"I don't understand."

"Lots of gasthauses, bahnhofs and such in Germany use these women to keep the bathrooms clean and to pass out little bars of soap, hand towels, lotions, etc. That lady in there is probably a relative or neighbor, and the folks here let her earn a little extra money by being a Latrine Frau. I know it doesn't sound like they are doing her a favor, but believe me they are. Times are still rough for most folks around here and she can at least help put food on their table by being a Latrine Frau. I don't know if you were in there long enough to notice or not, but there are no fixtures in there either. Just a small ditch in the floor close to the wall with a trickle of water running through it. That's the urinal. I wanted to bring you over here tonight to let you get a feel for the real rural Germany."

"How much tip?" Frank asked.

"I usually give her a couple of Marks or a hand full of Pfennigs, whatever I happen to have in my pocket."

"Thanks," and, Frank got up and went back to the bathroom.

Circa 1958 German Postcard

Top: Arial view of Hoppstädten. The white area at the top, just left of center near the hill is the 98th Hospital complex. The white tall building in the middle left of the photo is Höhn's Gasthaus and the old Luftwaffe air strip is across the road from the gasthaus.

Bottom Left: Höhn's Gasthaus. The lettering on the side of the building over the door reads *Gasthof Höhn*.

Bottom Right: Interior bar area of the gasthaus.

TWO

IT GETS COMPLICATED

"I have some news that's not going to make you very happy," Specialists Shipley said as he sat down in Major Bradley's office.

"What about?"

"Hans Müller. He is a Nazi, and he did poison Bill, but he is no Russian spy."

"And you know that for sure how?"

"I've been watching him now for over three months and during that time he has never done one thing even remotely suspicious. Unless you count hating Americans as being suspicious. When Bill came to Neubrücke he got here in the middle of the day and instead of reporting in he stopped by The Four Daughters. Maybe he knew something or suspected something I don't know, but while he was there one of those girls started flirting with him and he made a date with her for later that evening. Hans had already noticed his daughter's interest in the American and didn't like what was going on. When he overheard her talking to her sisters about having a date with the American Hans doctored the next beer that Erika brought to Bill. I don't know what he put in it, but I did overhear him one night talking to Fritz, another Nazi there in Neubrücke. He was bragging about all he was doing to the Americans. Especially any that tried to fool around with one of his girls. Bill wasn't poisoned by a spy ring. He was poisoned for trying to fool around with that old Nazi's daughter. He was somewhere he shouldn't have been, trying to do something he shouldn't have been doing, and unfortunately for him he met a German still fighting WW II and this time the German won that battle."

"That's kind of like the pot calling the kettle black, isn't it? With your reputation, I wouldn't be criticizing someone else for trying to fool around with the German girls. Do you have anything else for me?"

"I'm also beginning to have some concerns about this assignment."

"You mean about your assignment?"

"No, I mean about there even being a spy ring here. I've been snooping around here for over three months now and haven't seen or heard anything that would lead me to believe there are spies here. Why would there be? There's nothing of military importance, or of any other kind of importance here. Maybe over in Baumholder or at that tack air group over in Birkenfeld, but not here in this hospital. What in the world would be of interest to anyone in this back water outpost?"

"You getting tired of your assignment?"

"Not in the least. It's one of the easiest assignments I ever had. No work, no duty to speak of and all the good cheap beer and women a man could want. I don't mean the women are cheap, but they are good and willing. Claude and I are out most every night making the rounds of the gasthauses. Drinking beer with the women to get them loosened up so they will talk."

"Yeah sure. I don't doubt you are trying to loosen them up, but it's not talk you have on your mind. I've been receiving some reports about your and Claude's nightly patrols. You all are getting quite a reputation. When I told Claude to show you around, that was not what I had in mind."

"It's all been in the line of duty, sir! "

"For your information, there have been at least three more reports about this hospital and some of the incidents that have happened here sent to our friends over in East Germany since you've been here. I would suggest that you and Claude spend more time trying to find these people and less time chasing skirts. By the way, you can move back into the barracks."

The 6th CC barracks is in a three story masonry building they share with the 34th Ambulance Train. The building is connected to the main hospital complex by a breezeway, and the first floor contains the orderly rooms, supply rooms, company commanders offices and a couple of multiple use rooms. The thirty fourths' sleeping quarters are on the second floor and the 6th on the top floor. Since only about half of the thirty men now in the unit are quartered in the barracks only about half the space on the third floor is being used. In fact, only four rooms are being used. One for all the enlisted personnel under the rank of corporal and one for all the noncoms above the rank of E5. A third room is the living quarters for a master sergeant who is manager of the enlisted mens club and the fourth room is being used as a small rec room. However, the only equipment in it is a pool table. SP5 Frank Shipley moved back into the room with the other sergeants.

The breezeway provides protection from the weather and anyone living in the barracks has no need to ever leave the complex. There is a small PX and commissary, a snack bar, barber shop, theater, chapel and the main hospital dining room all located on the first floor in one wing of the hospitals main building. All the administrative and command offices for the hospital are in another wing. The hospital message center is located near the main entrance to the hospital next door to the hospital Sergeant Major's office. There is an O Club on the first floor of the BOQ, which is located, at the edge of some woods just up the hill from the main hospital building and an EM Club is located just down the hill from that near the back gate. The motor pool, shops, garages and supply buildings are located near the front gate, and the whole hospital complex is surrounded by a chain link fence topped with three strands of barbed wire angled away from the base. The hospital Provost Marshal's office and MP headquarters is near the front gate, and both gates are manned by MP's. The gates are seldom closed but anyone entering or leaving is stopped and has to show proper ID to the MP's. One could spend their entire deployment here without ever having a need to leave the hospital complex. However, Morelocke and Shipley seem to have a need since they are out almost every night.

When they arrived at Höhn's that evening the parking lot was full. The gasthaus was packed. It was the last night of Fasching and everyone wanted to get in the last few minutes of celebrating before the beginning of Lent. There were no empty tables left when Frank and Claude arrived and Hale and Jones invited them to sit at a table with them. They didn't see the two American women standing just inside the gasthaus bar area. Charlene and Jan were two army wives that lived upstairs at the gasthaus. Their husbands were part of the 506th Field Artillery Observation Detachment that was stationed at the small air strip just across the road from the gasthaus. Army L19 and L20 observation and spotter planes now used the small air field that had been home to a fighter squadron of German ME 109's during the war. The 506th was taking part in some war games ten kilometers away at Baumholder on this last weekend of the Fasching Celebration. Claude and Frank had seen these couples several times before this in the gasthaus and had even shared a few beers with them on several occasions. However, they were caught by surprise when the women came out from the bar area and plopped themselves down on their laps. There were no empty chairs left anywhere in the gasthaus. Claude and Frank spent an enjoyable evening dancing with and sharing beers with Charlene and Jan.

After Specialist Shipley left his office, Major Bradley turned and asked the gentleman that was sitting just on the other side of the door in another office what he thought?

"He's right about one thing, there is absolutely nothing of military importance or even of interest in that hospital. I also agree with him about there not being a spy ring here." Harold Sobel said.

"But, what about the reports your folks over in East Germany are sending back?"

"Oh, there's someone doing some snooping or spying here, but I believe he or she is acting alone. There's not a spy ring here. I think they may have gotten to someone or planted someone here and they're keeping them busy sending in those meaningless reports until something big happens or we get into another shooting war. Either way it's important enough to find out who is involved. If it is someone they got to and persuaded to work for them we need to find out how and why. If they planted one of theirs here, that's another ball game altogether."

"How so?"

"We need to find out what or who is so important for them to be that interested in this place. There's more going on here right now than meets the eye. How about your two agents, can they be trusted?"

"I think so, why?"

"There's been a lot of talk. It seems they are a lot more interested in what the German girls have to offer than finding Russian spies."

"They do have a reputation, and I have spoken to them about it."

"Maybe it's time you did more than just talk."

Harold Sobel is the senior CIA field agent in Germany. He had not been in favor of bringing the CID into this investigation, but his boss in Washington said that since the army was or might be involved the CID needed to be involved. They were also under a lot of pressure right now to improve interagency relationships and Harold had reluctantly agreed to let the CID agents come in. But, while it might appear he was cooperating he was going to keep the CID honest by keeping an eye on them. Claude and Frank may have thought they had just gotten lucky that night at Höhn's when Fasching ended, but Charlene and Jan were more than just a couple of army wives. They were working for the CIA. They had been recruited by Harold to watch and listen to what went on at Höhns when the reports first started showing up in East Germany. After his conversation with Bradley, Harold had asked the girls to also keep an eye on Claude and Frank, and if the opportunity came up to try and find out what they were all about. That's why after watching Claude and Frank for a few minutes that evening at Höhns they came out and sat down with them, and at midnight when the Fasching Celebration ended they agreed to go for a ride with them. They made no objections when after driving around for a while Claude parked on a hill overlooking Birkenfeld. It was time for them to go to work and get the information Harold wanted.

Harold was thirty five years old and the streaks of gray in his hair and the wrinkles in his face made him look much older. As a twenty year old platoon sergeant in the 1st Infantry Division Harold had crawled across much of this same Germany he now works in. In fact, as a boy he had played in some of these same woods before he and his parents escaped to America just before Hitler sent his army into Poland. Harold's Dad was a Jew and had owned a jewelry shop in nearby Idar Oberstein. The shop had been in the Sobel family for three generations. Josef Sobel and his family had barely escaped with their lives just before the Brownshirts came in one night and carried off what few gems and jewelry Josef had over looked the night before when he had cleaned out his shop. After ransacking the shop, they burned it and all the other shops owned by Jews in Idar Oberstein to the ground. Harold was only fourteen years old and had watched his dad cry as they were packing up the gems and jewelry.

Josef had been planning his escape for several months but had only told his family about it the week before. Although only fourteen years old, Harold had a much better understanding of what was happening in Germany than some of the adults did. He had watched from an upstairs window in their home over the shop while some of his friend's parents had been ridiculed and even beaten. He was not surprised at his Dad's announcement, but still it hurt to see him cry while they were cleaning out and packing up the inventory from the shop. What Harold didn't know was that for the past six months Josef had been selling off and reducing the store's inventory. He was only keeping back his most expensive gems and settings and what he thought he could easily conceal in their luggage. These he planned to use to start a new business once they were settled in America. Josef had planned to send Harold and his wife ahead to America with the majority of the gems, and he would follow later. However, the Brownshirts had shown up in Idar long before Josef was expecting them. A friend warned him that the Nazis were in town and Josef and his family was literally going out the back door as the Brownshirts were kicking in their front door. The Nazis were much more concerned that evening with destroying Jewish shops than capturing people and the Sobels were able to escape. Seeing the hurt and fear in his dads eyes that night while they were making their escape was more than Harold's fourteen year old heart could stand. He made up his mind that night if they made it to safety he would someday come back and finish the fight his dad wasn't able to. The family settled in East Tennessee near friends that had fled Germany the year before and shortly after graduating from high school Harold joined the army. After finishing advanced basic training at Fort Jackson, South Carolina, Harold was assigned to the 1st Infantry Division in England where they were getting ready for D Day.

Pvt Harold Sobel was a rifleman in the 2nd squad, 3rd platoon of Easy Company and three days after his nineteenth birthday he waded ashore on Omaha Beach with the second wave of the invasion. By the end of the day when the Big Red One had started moving inland Pvt Sobel had become a squad leader and promoted to corporal. There were only three men left in his squad out of the ten men that landed on the beach that morning. After the breakout from the beachhead the 1st Division drove across France, reaching the German border at Aachen, in September. The division laid siege to the city and after a bloody fight secured Aachen. They then continued East attacking through the Hurtgen Forest while driving to the Rur. After six months of continuous fighting the division was moved to a secure area in the rear on December 7 for a much needed rest and refitting. Corporal Sobel was promoted to sergeant and became the platoon sergeant of the 3rd platoon. He was one of only ten men left out of the original platoon that had waded ashore at Omaha Beach six months earlier. They had been promised a long rest, but Hitler had other plans. Someone forgot to tell the Germans the war was over and they launched the Wacht Am Rhein offensive on the 16th of December. In America, this fight was known as The Battle of the Bulge and after only two weeks rest and before what few replacements they got could be oriented the 1st Infantry division was quickly mobilized and sent to defend against the

German attack at the Ardennes front. That brief rest would be the only one they would get for the rest of the war. After blunting and reversing the German attack in the Ardennes, they went on the offensive and attacked and breached the Siegfried Line, fought on across the Ruhr and drove to the Rhine River. They crossed the Rhine at the Remagen bridgehead and after breaking out from the bridgehead took part in the encirclement of the Ruhr Pocket and captured Paderborn. From there, they pushed through the Harz Mountains and the Big Red One Division was in Czechoslovakia fighting at Kinsperk when the war ended. By the time his fight was over Sobel had become a master sergeant and had been awarded a silver star, a bronze star with two clusters, the combat infantry badge and the French Croix de Guerre. The one medal he didn't receive was a purple heart. The only combat related wound Sergeant Sobel received during WW II was a cut finger while using a P38 opener on a can of C rations.

Before the division was sent home the army was looking for German speaking Americans for assignments as interpreters during the roundup and trials of Nazi war criminals. Harold volunteered and found out he loved this almost as much as he did killing Germans during the war. When he finally did come home he learned the OSS was looking for German speaking Americans and Harold became an OSS agent. After six months of training Harold found himself once again in Germany. This time in the Russian Zone of East Germany gathering intelligence on troop movements and capabilities. He was one of the first agents to warn Washington of the Russian intent to completely seal off East Germany from the rest of the world. When the Iron Curtain descended across Europe he became an invaluable asset to the OSS. After President Truman created the CIA out of the OSS Harold spent two more years in East Germany both recruiting agents and gathering intelligence information. In 1956, he was brought out of East Germany and given field command of all agents in Europe.

He had been aware of spying activities in and around Neubrücke long before the army became involved. In fact, he had been the one to suggest the spies might be in the army and operating out of the 98th General Hospital. However, he had been puzzling for several months now as to why anyone would be gathering information or intelligence about a general hospital. Or for that matter, why would the Russians or East Germans be so interested in this rural back water nothing of a place in and around Neubrücke? It didn't make any sense to him, but he had been in this business long enough to know that when something didn't make much sense it was time to be careful. That's why he had assigned those two girls to keep an eye on the CID agents. Harold had learned the hard way a long time ago not to trust anyone when it came to spying. One of the first agents he had recruited in East Germany had turned out to be a double agent and had almost cost Harold his life and career. He wasn't about to make that mistake again.

Harold's assessment of the CID was that while they might be capable of conducting a criminal investigation within the army, they didn't know jack squat about spies. He had also heard some stories about Major Bradley. He wasn't about to trust them to turn up any spies at the 98th, and he wasn't about to let them screw up his investigation either. However, he was surprised when Charlene and Jan told him what they had learned that night in Claude's car on that hill overlooking Birkenfeld. Those two guys were a lot smarter than they let on or anyone gave them credit for. While it might appear all they were interested in was German beer and girls all that was just a cover. They knew a lot more than they let on, and if there were spies at the hospital Claude and Frank would likely know about it long before anyone else did. Harold hadn't asked what they had to do in order to get that information.

After bringing the girls back to Höhn's that night and seeing that they were safely inside Claude drove back to the hospital and pulled into the parking lot behind the 6th CC barracks and the two of them sat there smoking.

"What just happened?" Claude asked.

"I'm not sure, but I think we were just interrogated," Frank said.

"I get that feeling also, but why, and by whom?"

"I wish I knew. I didn't know what to think when you took that blanket and got out of the car."

"I didn't either," Claude said. "That was Charlene's idea. However, I assure you nothing more than some heavy breathing went on out there under that blanket. How about you, did you get any farther than first or second base?"

"I touched third a couple of times, but that's all. Those girls weren't interested in anything like that tonight. All they were interested in was getting some information." Frank said.

"Could those girls be the spies?" Claude asked.

"No way, I did some questioning of my own. They may be working for someone, but it's not the Russians. Those girls are as American Apple Pie as we are. Do you think it's Bradley?"

"No, I don't think he's smart enough nor has enough influence to have set something like that up."

"Maybe the CIA?" Frank asked.

"Could be, we know they were snooping around here long before we got involved. Are we being used?"

"I'm beginning to get that feeling."

"One thing I know for sure, there's no spy ring around here," Claude said.

"Yeah, I made the mistake of telling that to Bradley the other day."

"What did he say?"

"He told me to shut up and keep looking. What do we do now?"

"I guess we continue to act dumb and see where this goes. There's a lot more going on than we've been told."

"Well, one thing's for sure. I've never had so much fun working a case in my life," Frank said.

"Yeah, and to think we're getting paid to do this," Claude said.

The next morning when Morelocke got to his supply room Major Stovall the ninety eighths' Provost Marshal was waiting for him. What now Morelocke thought as he got out of his car.

"Good morning Major, what can I do for you?"

"What the hell is going on with my radios?"

"How should I know, I'm no radio expert?"

"You know damn well what I'm talking about. We've installed those new radios in every vehicle and none of them work. You know why?"

"I don't have the slightest idea."

"The hell you don't. None of them have the crystals in them."

"Your people didn't order any crystals. I ordered just what was on the requisition. I can pull it and show you if you would like to see it. I ordered six RFQ 9807J/mobile and one RFQ 9800M/base unit just like the requisition called for. There was nothing on that requisition about any crystals."

"Maybe not, but you knew they wouldn't be worth a damn without the crystals. Now what is going on? What kind of silly game are you playing?"

"Why don't you ask your people?"

"What do you mean?"

"I can't turn around without one of your cops on my ass about something. Every time I go in or out the gate they want to see pass or ID. I can't even enjoy a beer in a gasthaus any more without one of your cops coming in to check my ID. Hell, I can't even go to the latrine without one of them following me. You pull your people off my back and maybe those crystals will show up." Stovall stormed out of the supply room and got back in his jeep and left. "Sergeant Harrell, get in here," he yelled through the door after getting back to his office.

"What the hell is going on with Sergeant Morelocke?" And he explained what Morelocke had told him.

"I don't know anything about that."

"Well you better find out and get it straightened out. Whatever is going on is the reason we didn't get the crystals with our radios." Before Harrell could reply a corporal stuck his head in the door and said, "Colonel Hodge is on the phone for the Major." Stovall picked up the phone and after listening for a minute said, "Yes sir I'll be right there."

"I have to go see the Colonel," he said as he hung up the phone. "And when I get back I want some answers."

"Yes sir," Sergeant Harrell said and he saluted as he turned around and walked out of the office.

Sergeant Preston just smiled as the major walked into the office and said, "go on in he's expecting you."

"Do you know anything about this CID foolishness?" Hodge asked before the major was halfway through the door. Stovall had learned that Hodge expected answers and one of them better not be no.

"I'm sorry sir. I'm not aware of any CID activity around here," he said. Hodge then explained what he had heard and ordered the major to look into it.

"Well sir, don't you think if the CID wanted us to know what was going on they would have told us?" The minute the words were out of his mouth he knew he had said the wrong thing. Colonel Hodge turned beet red and Stovall thought he could see steam coming from his ears as he slowly got up and pointed a finger at the major.

"How dare you speak to me like that? I'm the troop commander here and have the right to know everything that goes on around here, and that includes any CID activity. You get your ass out of here and don't come back until you find out why they showed up in my command and started conducting an investigation without first notifying me. Is that clear?"

"Perfectly," Stovall said and saluted as he left the office. Pompous old fool he mumbled as he went out the door.

"What's going on?" he asked Preston

"I wish I knew. Somehow he heard talk about some CID agents being here and he's been like a wild man ever since. He even tried calling 7th Army Headquarters. Everyone he's talked to told him they didn't know what he was talking about. I was able to confirm that a sergeant Stevens had some medical problems as he was reporting in to the 6th CC and he might have been CID. The next day after he reported in and got sick a 7th Army major showed up and Smith introduced him to his orderly room as CID. That was after the major had Smith in Worley's office for a long time. That sergeant that got sick was under armed guard in ICU and now he's disappeared."

"What do you mean disappeared?"

"He's no longer here, and there is no record that he ever was here."

"No wonder the colonel is so upset."

"Yeah, well if you don't get some answers for him I'm afraid there's going to be hell to pay around here for a while."

When Stovall left the colonel's office he went looking for Larsen. PFC Larsen worked for SP5 Shipley in the message center and he knew a little of everything that went on in the hospital. If there was any CID activity Larsen would know about it. If Hodge had heard the rumors he was sure Larsen had also.

"Hey Major," Larsen said when Stovall walked up to the message center window. "You picking up the MP messages today?"

"No, I need some information. What do you hear about a possible CID investigation going on here in the hospital?"

"Not much. The scuttlebutt is that a CID agent was admitted to ICU a few months ago, but there is no record of that ever happening. Plenty of rumors circulating about different people seeing him and some even swearing he went to work in their section, but no one ever saw him."

"What do the folks in ICU say?"

"They say it never happened. However, I have a buddy that was on a special guard detail up there. He said they were armed and had orders to shoot to kill if anyone tried to get in that room. He watched them roll whoever was in that room out of there on a gurney and load him on a medevac helicopter. They were told not to talk about it."

"A lot of good that did I see. Thanks Larsen. If you see or hear anything else let me know."

"Will do," Larsen said. As the major was walking away he was mumbling to himself. I wonder how many other people around here know about this. Probably all of them by now. No wonder Hodge is so worked up.

After Stovall left the message center Shipley told Larsen he had an errand to run and would be gone for awhile.

"We just had an interesting visitor in the message center," he told Sergeant Morelocke as he walked into the supply room.

"Who would that be?" Morelocke asked.

"Major Stovall."

"He's sure getting around this morning. He was here waiting for me when I got to work this morning."

"He wasn't asking about this CID business I hope?"

"No, he wanted to chew my ass about crystals for his radios. What about the CID?"

"He came by the message center to see Larsen. He asked him what he knew about a CID investigation. Said that Hodge was asking about it."

"Shit! That's all we need is for that loser to get involved."

"I don't think he is involved. From what I could hear, Hodge has been hearing some rumors and has asked Stovall to find out what is going on."

"Then I'd say it's time we blew some smoke up their ass. Meet me in the snack bar in thirty minutes and we'll give them something to really talk about."

THREE

THE CIA AGENTS

S ergeant First Class Paul Lyons was one of the sergeants in the room Specialist Shipley moved back into with when he moved back into the barracks. Sgt Lyons was the hospital's food service supply sergeant. He was in charge of all the hospital's kitchen supplies, including buying the groceries. The army had long ago determined that it was much more efficient and economical to have one menu for each army area. That meant all the army units in Germany drew the same rations. How they were prepared and the order they were used was left to the discretion of each unit mess sergeant. However, at the 98th General Hospital when the dietitian made up the diet plans for the patients she also made out the menu for the main hospital mess hall. The soldiers at the hospital didn't eat by the same menu the rest of the army did. It was part of Sergeant Lyons job to take the menus and make out a grocery list. Then, instead of going to a battalion supply depot like the rest of the army mess sergeants did, Sgt Lyons went grocery shopping at the army commissary. For the soldiers at the hospital it was more like eating in a restaurant than an army mess hall. Lyons usually made one or two trips a week to the grocery store in Baumholder.

Sgt Lyons was one of the older men in the 6th CC and was a veteran of WW II. In fact, he had been a mess sergeant in a combat unit that had fought through this very area where he was now stationed. As they were getting ready for a Saturday morning barracks inspection shortly after Shipley moved back on base, he noticed the rows of ribbons on Lyons shirt. One of them was a Silver Star decoration. The next time they were out making the rounds of the gasthauses Frank told Paul he wanted to ask him a couple of questions. Paul told him he might or might not answer the questions, but to go ahead and ask.

OK, Frank said, "for starters, I think you have been in the army for fifteen or sixteen years."

"Seventeen, going on eighteen. What about it?" Lyons said.

"Why after all that time are you only a Sergeant First Class?"

"I've been a Master Sergeant several times. The last time was before I came up here when one of the platoon leaders in my company made some disparaging remarks about my kitchen. I told him if he thought he could run it any better he could have the job. Then I threw my cooks cap at him and left. When I got back a couple of days later the CO took a couple of my stripes and said if it happened again he would bust me all the way back to private. I'll be a Master again before I retire though."

"I'm sure you will. My other question is about that Silver Star medal you have."

"What about it?"

"You told me you had been a cook during the war."

"That's right."

"How does a cook go about getting awarded a Silver Star?"

"By being somewhere he had no business being. It was near the end of the war and things had been quiet for a couple of days. I was the headquarters company mess sergeant and running a battalion mess. One afternoon I borrowed a jeep and went up to the front where one of our line companies was to visit a friend. While I was there the Germans decided to launch a counter attack. The company was being overrun and before I could get the jeep turned around and bug out I was surrounded. I climbed up in the back of the jeep and started using the 50 caliber machine gun that was mounted there to defend myself. I wasn't trying to win any medals. I was scared shitless and was determined to kill as many of them as I could before they killed me. They said my action inspired the company to fight back and what I did gave them time to regroup and turn back the attack. I wasn't a hero and told them so. I was only trying to save my ass. But, they gave me the medal anyway."

A few days later as they were getting ready for the day Paul started putting on his class A uniform instead of the cooks whites he usually wore and said, "I'll see you in a couple of days." As they were walking up the corridor to the mess hall that morning Frank asked Claude what that was all about.

"I think that may be one of the reasons Lyons is no longer a Master Sergeant."

"What do you mean?"

"He goes off like that ever once in a while. I don't know where or what, and he comes back in two or three days. Usually hung over and missing part of his uniform."

"What about his job?"

"WO Jacobs covers for him. Since we don't have reveille or roll call Sergeant Smith or Captain Worley never know he's gone."

"What would happen if we had an alert one of those times while he is gone?"

"Then I think he might be in real trouble, but so far he's been lucky. He goes off like this about once a month or so. The rest of the time he's one of the best soldiers here."

The alerts were 7th Army's way of reminding everyone there was still a real danger of war with the Russians and to keep a check on the readiness of the army units in Germany to face such a challenge. All army units in Germany had battle ready positions they were supposed to man and be ready to face the enemy if the threat were real. The combat units along the line between East and West Germany had gun positions and fortifications they reported to and their standing orders were to hold at all cost for as long as they could. The rest of the units in Germany had fall back positions and evacuation routes they were supposed to use in case of attack. When an alert was called all army personnel reported to their defensive positions as soon as possible and prepared for combat. Specialists Shipley's orders were to report to the message center and destroy all non essential papers and equipment and get the rest ready to move to their fallback position. This was to a hospital somewhere near the coast of France. Sergeant Morelocke was to report to his supply room and load all equipment that was designated for the move onto trucks and prepare to destroy the rest.

The alerts usually happened in the middle of the night or just before daylight. Fortunately, so far they had all just been a drill. At least up until that one last month. President Eisenhower had ordered the army to intervene in Lebanon in what became known as Operation Blue Bat to enforce the Eisenhower Doctrine. This was a policy of the US government under Eisenhower to support and protect any nation the US considered vital to US interest from Communists takeover. When US troops landed at the Beirut airport the 7th Army went on alert. When the medical personnel at the 98th Hospital reported for duty that morning, three doctors and two nurses were sent to a MASH unit in the 24th Division which was being deployed to Lebanon.

Ever since he could remember Harold had used the protestant church that was embedded in the rock cliff 200 feet above the Nahe River in Idar Oberstein as a quiet place to go and think. According to legend the church had been built in the 12th century by an Oberstein resident as atonement for a fratricide. The Idar valley has been famous for centuries for its agate industry. Since the 18th century, however, the stone cutters have concentrated on cutting, polishing and coloring semi precious stones sent to the region from other parts of the world. That is why the Sobel Jewelry shop was located there before the war. Even though his family were Jews Harold had used the protestant church as a sanctuary every since he was old enough to climb the long staircase up the sheer rock wall to get to it. That, along with the fact that he had grown up in this area of Germany was the reason he had chosen Idar for his headquarters. Another reason was his taste for Spiessbraten. He couldn't wait to get back to the area after the war and see if they were still serving this delicious pork dish. The area in and around Idar was the only place in Germany one could find this delicacy. A pork loin split open, stuffed with red cabbage and cooked slowly over a pit was said to have been originated by some men from Idar who went to Brazil in search of diamonds. This tasty pork dish has been a specialty of the region ever since. Harold was pleasantly surprised to find the gasthauses in and around Idar still preparing and serving Spiessbraten and that it was just as good as he remembered. He was sure his Dad had never tasted any of that pork, but Harold wasn't as orthodox as his Dad and had learned how delicious that flame broiled pork dish was while eating supper at the home of one of his friends. Today after coming back from his meeting with Major Bradley he had enjoyed a nice Spiessbraten dinner washed down with a local beer. Now he needed some quiet time to think. Something about Major Bradley and this whole spy business was bothering him.

It seemed there were more steps, and the climb up the wall was a lot steeper than he remembered as a boy, but the view of the town and the valley beyond from the church balcony and the peace he found while sitting there made the climb worth it. Maybe it was time he started using the other entrance to the church. The one most others used. The one that came down the short distance from the top of the cliff. Something about that major and the whole spy business in Neubrücke was troubling him. Something wasn't right about the whole CID thing. Those two agents, Claude and Frank for instance. They wanted everyone to believe they were dumb and only interested in chasing German girls. It wasn't like that at all. What was it Charlene and Jan had told him about them? Together they probably had more sense than all the other CID agents in Germany combined. Now as he sat there and thought about it he wondered what their game was. As for spies, Harold was sure there was no ring here. He didn't know that Claude and Frank had also come to that conclusion. However, he couldn't just ignore the fact that something was going on. Someone was sending meaningless reports about that hospital to the East Germans. Who would be doing that and why? That's what kept nagging at him. Why? There had to be a reason. These people weren't stupid and wouldn't risk their network and communications systems for these meaningless reports. There had to be a reason they were willing to take that risk and he had to get to

the bottom of it. It was time to bring someone else into the game. This
was beginning to take more of his time away from his coordinating the
activities of the other agents than he could afford right now. It was time
to send for Jess, and while he was at it he would have someone do a good
background check on Bradley.

Jess Millsap had grown up in the mountains along the Tennessee and North
Carolina border following his uncle around looking for ginseng. When
the war started he joined the Army Air Corps and was sent to Camden,
South Carolina for basic training. After he finished basic flight training
he was sent to Bush Field in Augusta, Georgia for primary flight training.
After learning to fly a Stearman PT 19, he was sent to Barksdale Field in
Louisiana for more training. He had applied for fighter training, but was
selected to be a bomber pilot instead, and sent to McDill Air Force Base
in Tampa Florida to learn to fly a Boing B 17 Flying Fortress. Jess found,
like so many other new pilots did, that the B 17 was a dream to fly. They
would soon learn that it not only was a dream to fly but would continue
flying after having been shot to pieces by the German fighter planes. Jess
was sent to England's Duxford Air Field and assigned to the 91st Bomb
Group, 324th Bombardment Squadron, 8th Bomber Command.

Jess's military career almost ended with his first mission. His plane was
so badly damaged from flak and 20 mm cannon shells during a raid on
the sub pens on the northern coast of Germany it was hardly recognizable
as a plane. Most of the rudder had been shot away and the stabilizer was
in shreds. Both wings were riddled with holes and one engine had been
almost torn off the wing. There was a gaping hole in the fuselage where the
top gun turret had been and the plexiglas nose was riddled with holes from
20 mm cannon shells. Somehow the plane continued to fly, but it took all
the strength Jess had to keep it under control. They were steadily losing
altitude, and about half way back across the English Chanel another engine
failed. The copilot suggested they bail out. Lt. Millsap told him no way.

"I'm not about to have to swim back to England," he said. "And besides, we have several dead and wounded men back there. If at all possible, I'm going to see that those still alive have a chance of making it. As long as this plane continues to fly we're staying with it."

He landed about fifty yards from the coast on the first flat piece of ground he saw. Millsap's luck held, and after completing thirty five missions he was reassigned to McDill Air Force Base in Florida to train new pilots to fly the B 17. Long before the war was over Captain Millsap had made up his mind to remain in the air corps. Three months after the war ended he was promoted to major and sent back to Germany to Rhine-Main Air Force Base as commander of a bomber wing in the US Army's Air Defense Command.

No other country was devastated more than Germany at the end of the war. The allied bombing raids had been merciless during the war. Not only destroying most of Germany's factories and industries, but most of their infrastructure as well. Most cities of any size in Germany were in total ruins when their war ended in 1945. Disease was everywhere in the country and winter was about to set in. Most Germans had been on rations for seven years and their rations were being cut even more after the war. Most were on the brink of starving to death. Then, the coldest winter on record in the previous hundred years set in threatening to wipe out their entire population. Major Millsap organized and helped oversee a relief effort made up of a group of his fellow flyers. They began to beg, borrow and sometimes steal food and supplies and distribute them to the Germans in the surrounding villages and towns. On one of these distribution trips Jess recognized the name of one of the towns they visited as being one of their secondary targets one day when their primary had been obscured by clouds. He couldn't wait to look round, and then he saw the church and school. An old man was picking through some debris around the bombed out school. Jess was trying to talk to him and getting nowhere when one of the other pilots asked if he could help. "I speak some German," he said.

"Ask him if he lived here before the war?" Jess said. When told the answer was yes he said, "Ask him if there were children in the school when it was bombed?" The old German talked for a long time and gestured towards the ruined buildings and the ground. There were tears in the pilot's eyes when he turned back to Jess.

"The children had been told by the nuns they would be safe in the school building," he told Jess. "When the bombs started coming down that day most of them didn't make it out of the building. They are buried in a mass grave out behind what remains of the school building along with all the others that were killed that day. A priest, some nuns who were the school teachers and others. One of the children he buried that day was his only son."

Jess stood there in stunned silence for a long time looking at the bombed out buildings and the old man, then ran from the town screaming. When they got back to the air field he went in the first bar he came to and had to be carried out when the bar closed at curfew. He never flew again.

He resigned his commission just before they were going to boot him out of the Air Force, and returned to the mountains of East Tennessee where he had grown up. It took him almost a year before he could make it through the day without a drink. One day in one of his rare lucid moments he saw an ad in a magazine. The words seemed to jump off the page at him. WANTED – Ex-military personnel for exciting and sometimes hazardous work for the government. Excellent pay, benefits and world travel. If you think you have what it takes to be one of us apply at your nearest US Post Office. Jess tore out the page with the ad and took it the next day to the post office building in Roan Mountain. He showed the ad to the post master and was handed an application. He filled it out on the spot. He knew he would have to be sober and dried out if they sent for him and he vowed to go on the wagon that day. Three weeks later the letter he was looking for came and a now sober Jess Millsap drove over to Johnson City and met with the OSS representative. The address the letter gave was for one of the lecture rooms in the science building at East Tennessee State College and there were already about a dozen other young men there when Jess arrived. Most of them were college students that had been recruited there at the school. The OSS rep started off by explaining what the program the government was offering was all about and what the challenges and benefits would be if they were accepted and qualified for the job. He told them they would be given a battery of written and oral tests and those that qualified would be sent to a secure and secret location for six months of training. After they completed that they would then spend another three to six months of further training by actually accompanying an agent in the field on real cases. During that time they would have absolutely no contact with family or former friends. He then offered anyone that didn't want to continue with the program a chance to leave. About half the students got up and left.

For the next nine months Jess had been put through some of the most rigorous testing and training exercises he had ever experienced. Then for the next five years Jess had been: An ESSO oil worker in Saudi Arabia looking for a saboteur. A Gaucho in Argentina working with an Israeli Mossad agent looking for Nazis. An American Embassy clerk in Moscow looking for an imposter working in the embassy. An American exporter in Australia looking for terrorists. An oiler on a freighter looking for weapons smuggling. A marine guard at the American Embassy in Beijing, China listening for any info about Chairman Mayo's Red Brigade. And, a state department employee in West Germany looking for army deserters and former Nazis. Somewhere along the way while all this was going on President Truman changed their name from Office of Strategic Services to the Central Intelligence Agency. Their mission remained the same. Gather intelligence outside the United States that could be vital to US security. They were free to gather intelligence in any foreign country, but not to conduct any covert operations within the borders of the continual US.

It was during his German assignment where Jess first met Harold Sobel. He had been assigned to work with Harold and they became instant friends. One of Harold's jobs at this time was recruiting Germans for assignments in East Germany. After working with one of these recruits for a while Jess became suspicious and had started keeping an eye on the recruit without Harold knowing about it. One night in a gasthaus Jess overheard the German passing on some information to another man and then being told it might be time to eliminate the American. Jess told Harold what he had seen and heard and they set a trap. It was the first time Jess had actually witnessed someone being killed. It had all happened so quickly and all Jess saw was the German falling to the ground and lying there as they ran away. Harold was afraid Jess' cover had been compromised and had him sent back to the states the next day.

After a brief rest, Jess was sent to Korea as an inspector for the various rebuilding projects the American government had started after that war. Jess was looking for North Korean spies posing as construction workers. Although Jess had by now been all over the world on under cover assignments he had never experienced any close calls. That all came to an end one night when he barely escaped with his life when one of the North Koreans he had been sent to find opened fire on the sleeping construction workers. Jess was returning from a night on the town and had just started to open the barracks door when the gunfire started. He ran for cover in a building next door. Some MP's just happened to be making their rounds when the shooting started and killed the North Korean assassin. For several weeks after that he was afraid to go to sleep at night.

After returning to the states he had been sent to Puerto Rico to help the FBI investigate a smuggling operation. Someone was bringing untaxed rum into Florida. Jess had been sent in because the FBI men were all too well known. Jess' job was to infiltrate the gang and set up a sale so the FBI could catch them in the act. Something went wrong, and when Jess went one night to talk to some of the smugglers one of them started shooting as soon a Jess got out of his car. Jess had no choice but to defend himself and the young man was killed. The young man had no sooner hit the ground when the night erupted with gunfire. The FBI men that were following Jess had opened fire and most of the smugglers and one of the FBI men was killed. It was the only up close and personal gun fight Jess had ever been in. He hoped it would be the last.

After Harold had picked Jess up at the Rhine-Main Airport in Frankfurt he stopped at the first gasthaus they came to.

"You look like you could use a beer," Harold said.

"Does it show that much?" Jess said. After they got their beers Harold asked Jess what went wrong?

"Have you been talking to Jim?"

"He told me some of it, but I want to hear your side."

"There's not a whole lot to tell. Something went terribly wrong. No one was supposed to get hurt. I guess Jim told you about the case I was working on."

"Yes he did."

"Well, when I went to talk to them that night for some reason as soon as I got out of the car a young man came out of the house and started shooting. I had to defend myself. It was the first time in all these years I've had to use my weapon. That young man was only twenty years old."

"You've killed before."

"I know, but I never had to look at their faces or watch them die. Sitting in that cockpit twenty thousand feet up in the sky I couldn't see what was happening down on the ground. I guess deep down I knew people were dying, but I didn't think much about that then. All I was interested in was whether those little black puffs of smoke outside were going to come crashing through my plane and riddle my body with pieces of shrapnel or if when I turned for home those ME 109s or Focke-Wulfs would be waiting for me. All I cared about was getting back to the base in one piece. Getting that plane back on the ground and getting a good drink at the O Club and a hot meal was all I cared about. It didn't matter that people were dying. It was war and people die in a war. I didn't realize what we did until I came back over here after the war and saw the damage. One of those towns I dropped bombs on was totally destroyed. Not just the factories and military stuff, but apartments, houses, a church and a school. I broke down and cried. I couldn't imagine what those kids must have thought when those bombs came down. Bombs that I had been responsible for dropping. It wasn't until then that it dawned on me. In a war it's not just soldiers that get killed. Lots of times innocent little kids also die, and I had been responsible for dropping the bombs that killed them. I stayed drunk for almost a year getting over that. I was just getting used to living with myself without all that guilt when I had to shoot that kid. Looking at his face and watching him die brought back the memory of that bombed out school house and I lost it. The next thing I remember is waking up on the nut ward at Walter Reed."

"Are you going to be ok?" Harold asked.

"With the help of those shrinks and a lot of little white pills the doc says I'm good to go. What did Jim tell you?"

"He said you needed to get back in the field as soon as possible and thought some time with me might be just what the doctor ordered. He wanted to get you out of that hospital and away from Washington as soon as possible. He also told me something else. You were set up that night in Puerto Rico. Hoover had planned that operation as an experiment to see how well our two agencies could work together. One of the FBI agents you were working with was upset that you were there. He thought he should have been given the undercover assignment and had sold you out. The smugglers knew who you were and why you were coming to see them that night. You were walking into an ambush. If that kid hadn't panicked and ran out of the house and started shooting you would have been the one laying there dead. That's why Jim wanted to get you back in the field so soon. He thinks you are too good of an agent to waste. So do I."

"OK, what's so urgent over here to get me out of that nice cozy hospital room?"

"Spies," Harold said.

"Spies?" Jess asked.

"Some of our friends over in East Germany have been intercepting reports from someone in or around the 98th General Hospital at Neubrücke. I didn't have anyone available so I started doing some snooping around there myself. However, somehow the CID got wind of what was going on and said since the army was involved it should be their investigation. They sent a Major Bradley over here to look into it. Ever hear of him?"

"I don't think so."

"Well consider yourself lucky. He thinks there is a gang or ring of spies involved and has convinced Washington and the 7th Army there is. I don't think so. I think there are only one or maybe two folks involved in what has been going on. However, whoever it is has been giving some very detailed reports about that hospital and the surrounding community to the East Germans. Most of the stuff they've been getting is not important enough to warrant a major concern, but it does have Washington and the 7th Army worried. None of what they've gotten so far is of any military importance, but the fact that they've been able to get it and give it to the commies is. That's why we need to find out who they are and shut them down."

"Why am I here?" Jess asked.

"I need you to take over this investigation so I can get back to the business of running the CIA's spook affairs in Germany. From now on you are Jeff McReynolds. You work for the state department and are here to check on the hospital's efficiency and capabilities. I have provided you with a history in case someone gets nosey and I've made arrangements for you to be billeted in the hospitals BOQ. From now on this spy business is all yours. You will have to cooperate or work with Bradley, and how you handle that is your business. You will also have to deal with Colonel Hodge. He's the ninety eighth's troop commander and is a pompous ass hole that's been promoted about two ranks above his capabilities. He loves to show his importance and is not very well respected or liked by the personal there, officer or enlisted. It is my understanding that he knows nothing about the spies, but has heard rumors of CID investigators in his hospital and is turning the place upside down trying to find out what's going on. My advice is don't give him any more information than you absolutely have to. You will also have membership in both the O Club and the EM Club. The O Club is located on the first floor of the BOQ and the EM Club is just down the hill from it. Both places will probably be excellent sources of information about what is going on in the hospital."

"Bradley has two agents working undercover in the hospital and they may be the burr under Hodge's saddle," Harold continued. "He doesn't know who they are or what is going on. Those two agents like to have everyone think they are dumb and are only interested in beer and girls. It's not like that at all. That's just a cover for them and, in my opinion, they are probably a lot more capable than Bradley or anyone else for that matter give them credit for. I don't know how much they have learned about the spies, and I get the feeling they don't think much of Bradley or his capabilities. I don't think much of Bradley either. Something about that man bothers me and I have asked Jim to do a background check on him. I'll let you know what I find out. Those two agents of his will probably make good allies for you. One is Sergeant Morelocke. He is the hospital's supply sergeant. The other one is SP5 Shipley, and he runs the hospital's message center. How you get to know them and how much you tell them about your job here is up to you, but I would suggest the sooner you get to know them the better. The beer here is fantastic, and I hear the German girls are real cooperative. I don't know about the nurses. You'll have to find that out for yourself. Welcome aboard Jeff."

"Whoa! You're sure dumping a load on a washed up old bomber pilot."

"I don't think so. You got the job after Jim told me what was going on. If I wasn't sure you could do the job you wouldn't be here. I wouldn't have let them send you over here. You deserve another chance. If anyone can do this job it's you. Of that I'm certain. Besides that, I owe you one. You saved my bacon back there that night in Essen. Now it's my turn to do you a favor. Joe Collins will be your driver and he will be waiting outside the BOQ at 0900 tomorrow morning. If you need to get in contact with me there is a phone number somewhere in all that mess of papers I gave you.

However, the phone lines are not secure, even the private in house phone service in the hospital. Have Joe get a message to me if it needs to be for my eyes and ears only. Good hunting.

FOUR

THE IG INSPECTION

"I have a problem," Frank said as he pulled up a chair and sat down across from Claude's desk.

"What kind of problem?"

"Smith asked me to do some investigating for him."

"What makes Smith think that you are an investigator?"

"The day I reported in he asked me if I was working for Bradley. Maybe I should have lied to him, but I didn't."

"What made him ask?"

"The orders I was carrying. They were same as the ones Bill had given him the day before."

"Anyone else know about this?"

"About him asking me to do some investigating, or that I'm CID?"

"Both."

"I don't think so."

"What has he asked you to do?"

"He says there are some supplies missing."

"Why doesn't he let Stovall handle it?"

"I asked him about that and he said it was something the CID should take care of. I agree with him. Investigating stuff like that is what I was trained to do, not this counterspy shit."

"Are you going to tell Bradley about this?"

"Hell no. If I do investigate, and something is going on I don't want him involved. I've learned that it's sometimes a lot easier and better to ask for forgiveness than to try and get permission"

"You're asking for trouble. With Bradley, you never know which way he's going to go."

"That's why I've come to you."

"Oh no, you're not dragging me into this."

"OK. If I do get involved, will you at least supervise like you did that time back there at Gordon?"

"Yeah, I might be able to do that. What's going on?"

"As you know we have an IG inspection coming up. Rollins was making sure his records were up to date, and during an inventory he found that his count was way off. Smith thought their records were messed up, but no such luck. The items are missing. Paul also reported some shortages in his kitchen inventory. Smith doesn't want the MP's involved because he wants more than an armed guard. He wants to find out who's involved, and why. He wants me to do some snooping around on the QT."

"OK, I'll cover for you on this spy business for a while. You better hope Bradley doesn't find out what's going on."

Frank soon learned that the 6th CC wasn't the only unit involved. The 34th Ambulance Train was missing some C Rations. They kept an inventory of the rations on hand to keep their unit, and all the patients the train could carry fed for up to five days in case there was an attack and they had to evacuate. About a fourth of their inventory was missing. The 98th supply room had also been hit and was missing some of the same items as the 6th CC. When Claude heard all this, he did a quick survey and found that he was also missing several items. The command was facing an IG inspection in two weeks. No way could the missing items be replaced in time.

The five supply sergeants had to come up with a plan, and fast. Paul said he could replace his items with a trip to the commissary, and by some horse trading with a buddy in Baumholder he thought he could also replace the thirty fourth's supply of C rations. That gave Shorty, the ninety eighth's supply sergeant, an idea. Why didn't they all see if they could do some wheeling and dealing with the units in Baumholder to replace most of their items. Then, with some sleight of hand maneuvering on the day of the inspection they might just squeak by. If they could find out which unit would be inspected first they would make sure their inventory was correct. Then, as soon as that inspection was over any items the second unit in line needed would be sneaked to them, and so on until all the units had been inspected. They all agreed it could work.

While all this was going on Stovall found out about it and insisted the MP's get involved. Both Smith and "Shakey", the ninety eighth's First Sergeant, told him all they needed from the MP's was an armed guard on the supply rooms until after the inspection. They didn't want the thieves scared off, they wanted them caught and having a bunch of MP's around wouldn't get that job done. Stovall agreed, but left the door open to revisit the issue after the inspection.

Major Alison and Lieutenant Conant, the IG inspectors, didn't have a clue they had looked at and counted the same items three different times while looking at the records in the different supply rooms. The IG Inspection went off without a hitch, and Colonel Hodge's command received an excellent rating. Colonel Hodge wasn't told about the thefts and the bait and switch scheme the supply sergeants pulled off until after the inspection. While Major Stovall was briefing him about the situation, Frank was already at work looking for the thieves.

He didn't like what he was finding. It wasn't going to be a local matter like he thought, and he was going to have to bring in Major Bradley after all. In discovering who the crooks were at the hospital he had really opened up a can of worms. What started out as the theft of some supplies at a remote army hospital had turned into a drug cartel and black market gang reaching all the way into East Germany, and back to the states. Bradley went through the roof and threatened to have Frank court martialed for not telling him what was going on in the beginning. Frank let him rant and rave until he ran out of steam, and then laid it all out for him. He wasn't brought in from the beginning because Frank hadn't expected it to go this far. It was supposed to only be a local matter not requiring much of his time. Bradley bought his explanation and agreed to let Frank continue to do the local leg work and he would take care of all the rest.

Frank learned the thefts were being committed to help some of the local economies in East Germany, and to buy drugs for distribution at the hospital. Two PFC's from the 98th and two local Germans that worked on the base were stealing the supplies and pawning them to a German supplier in Baumholder. He in turn sold them on a widespread black market network that was distributing the supplies in East Germany. The Russians didn't like to admit what a mess they were making in their occupation zone or that the East German economy was even worse than at the end of the war. The black market items being distributed in East Germany was all that was keeping some people alive. The agent in Baumholder used the proceeds from the black market sales to buy drugs from a dealer in Frankfurt. Two Master Sergeants flying back and forth from New Jersey to Frankfurt with the MATS flights were bringing in the drugs. Mostly amphetamines and marijuana that was being sold at the hospital. Frank turned all the information he had over to First Sergeant Smith. Smith gave the information to Stovall, who couldn't believe what he had been handed.

Major Stovall knew there was some drug use at the hospital, but couldn't believe that it was as wide spread as Frank had found, or that stolen supplies were being used as part of the payoff. Major Bradley had coordinated the CID's investigations in Baumholder and Frankfurt. When he submitted his report to 7th Army Headquarters no mention was made of Frank's involvement in the successful outcome of the investigations. General Johnson, the 7th Army's commanding general, had a commendation that contained more BS than the Chicago stock yards placed in Bradley's 201 file.

"Congratulations," Claude told Frank. "You may have just gotten Bradley that promotion he wants."

"Go to hell," Frank said. "I didn't do what I did for rewards or to get anyone promoted. I did it for two reasons. First, because Smith asked me to, and second, because doing something like that is why I became a CID agent in the first place. It's what I was trained to do"

"Are you ready to get back in the counterspy business?"

"No, but I guess I have to, don't I. Anything important happen while I was away?"

"No.

When Major Stovall got back to his office he asked Sergeant Harrell what he had found out about the problem with Morelocke.

"He was right about being harassed," Harrell told him. "One evening Morelocke had picked up Jimmy's girl at Höhns and took her to that gasthaus in the woods there near Birkenfeld. One of our patrols saw them and told Jimmy about it. That's what started the whole thing. Some of the other guys thought they should help out a friend, and that's why they've been dogging Morelocke."

"You mean I can't use my radios because Sergeant Tyler thought Morelocke might have laid his girl?"

"Looks like it."

"I can't believe this. Find out who all's been involved in this shit and get them in here."

"Yes sir. But, I think you might want to hear what else I found out?"

"What?"

"Up at the snack bar a while ago I overheard Morelocke and Shipley talking. According to them there is a CID agent here to investigate Colonel Hodge for incompetence and dereliction of duty."

"What? Do you believe that?"

"After I left the snack bar I went by to see Larsen and he confirmed it. He said he saw the message when it came through."

"That's what Hodge wanted to see me about. He ordered me to find out what was going on. I'm not about to tell him that he is the reason for the CID being here. Call Preston and set me up a meeting with the good

Colonel." Stovall was beginning to wonder if he should have a talk with Frank and Claude.

FIVE

NOW THE FUN BEGINS

hen Jeff came out of the BOQ the next morning Joe was just pulling in. After parking, Joe got out and said, "Good morning Mr. McReynolds," as he was opening the back door.

"Close the door. I don't ride in the back," Jeff said, and he walked around to the other side of the car, opened the door and slid in the front passenger seat. "Also," he said as Joe was getting back in the car, "It's Jeff, not Mr. McReynolds."

"OK Jeff. Where are we going this morning?"

"Just start driving. I want to get the lay of the land. You can tell me about it while we're driving around."

"Is this your first trip to Germany?" Joe asked as he pulled away from the BOQ and headed down the hill.

"Yes," Jeff lied.

"I think you will like it here. It's a nice and quiet little part of Germany. Not much excitement around here. That's the EM Club there on the right," Joe said as he went out the gate and turned left towards Birkenfeld.

"Birkenfeld is about five clicks from here. It is one of the largest and oldest towns in the area. However, that's not saying a lot where size is concerned. There is a small military presence there. The 7424th Tactical Air Squadron is located there. I think it's some kind of communications unit." As they drove through Birkenfeld Joe told Jeff that one of the oldest cities in Germany was Trier which was located about thirty clicks away to the northwest. Karl Marx the founder of communism was born and studied there.

Trier is the oldest city in Germany, and one of the most interesting. Trebeta, the founder of Trier, started the town thirteen hundred years before Rome was built. In fact, this beautiful valley in the southwestern corner of Germany was colonized three thousand years before Christ. Julius Caesar was the first Roman leader to enter Trier in 85 BC. Trier is a museum of European history, containing Roman ruins still in existence. An amphitheater, built by Trajan dates back to the second century, and is the oldest building in the city. The Porta Nigra, the largest gate ever constructed is still standing over the ancient streets. A cathedral there guards the Holy Mantle, believed to be the shroud in which Christ's body was wrapped. During the fourth century Trier was often the residence of Roman Emperors, and later became the seat of the powerful Archbishops of Treves. In 1794, the territory where Trier is located came under French control and was made the capital of the department of Saar. With the fall on Napoleon it passed to Prussia. Trier is an important rail center, a manufacturing town for leather and tobacco, and as a hub for the wine trade for the choicest vintages of the Mosel, Saar and Ruwer districts. There are fifty wine factories in Trier. Karl Marx, the founder of Communism was born and studied there, and in spite of the Nazi purge during WW II there is still a strong communist population and influence in the town. It is a hotbed of espionage in this southwestern corner of Germany.

As they drove out of Birkenfeld and headed up the hill Joe explained that the gasthaus in the edge of the woods was the Edelweiss and the only one in the area that is in an old farm house. "I think it's one of the nicest also. Being out of the way like it is it's never very crowded, and there's usually more Germans using it than GI's. The little village up ahead there is Dienstweiler. The road to the left takes you to Idar Oberstein, and the road to the right goes back over the hill towards Hoppstädten and Neubrücke."

When they got to Hoppstädten and Joe started talking about Baumholder Jeff told him to take him there.

The little town of Baumholder was located on top of a small flat hill. Joe explained that when the Nazis began their military buildup in the late 1930's they built a barracks and troop drilling ground there. In order to do this they displaced several hundred inhabitants. Not just from the little village, but from hundreds of acres of the flat grassland surrounding the town. During WW II the drilling ground was a POW camp. At the end of the war French soldiers were stationed there, and in 1951 the US Army took over the camp and built it up into one of the largest troop garrisons in Germany. This also brought the little town of Baumholder a lot of publicity it didn't want when brothels began springing up all over town. Countless sex trade workers began offering their services to the ready and willing American GI's. Baumholder soon became known all over the Western Command as a moral disaster area.

After leaving Baumholder, Joe drove back through the little town of Heimbach and finally back to Neubrücke, pointing out Höhn's and The Four Daughter's Gasthauses and telling Jeff those were the most popular hangouts for the hospitals GI's. However, instead of turning into the hospital he drove on about a kilometer to the west to the Saar border. "The Saar did not exist as a unified entity until its creation as a buffer between France and Germany by the League of Nations after WW I," Joe explained. "There was an almost immediate dispute over ownership by both the French and German governments due to the area's rich coal and mineral deposits. For ten years following WW II Saarland was occupied by the French. When the inhabitants were offered their freedom in 1955 they voted instead to become a German state. Even though the Saar is now a part of Germany it is not part of the occupied territory and the army's jurisdiction ends here at the border," Joe then turned the car around and drove them back to the hospital.

"Thank you for a very interesting tour," Jeff said. When they got back to the BOQ Jeff told Joe to take the rest of the day off. "In fact, I'll let you know the next time I need you. I want to do some exploring around in the hospital for the next few days. How do I go about getting in touch with you when I need you again?"

"Tell the bar tender in the O Club," Joe said and he drove off.

After Joe drove off Jeff went in the O Club and ordered a sandwich and beer. Something about Joe was bothering him. He couldn't put his finger on it, but the way Joe had taken charge after he told him to call him by his first name and his description of the area they had driven through was troubling him. It was the accent for one thing. Jeff was sure it wasn't German. Oh well he thought, it's probably just my imagination. After finishing his sandwich he decided to take a walk through the hospital. Walking down one of the hallways he saw a sign on one of the doors that read Colonel Hodge, and he thought why not and went in.

"May I help you?" Sergeant Preston asked.

"I'm Jeff McReynolds from the state department and would like a word with the Colonel if he is available."

"I don't think he has anything going on right now. Let me see if he can see you?"

The red head in the next office looked up and smiled at Jeff as Preston walked through to the colonel's office. Jeff smiled back and started to say something to her just as Preston came back through the office and said, "The Colonel will see you." He couldn't remember where he had learned that little trick of surprise visits when you actually didn't want to see or talk with someone. Throws them off balance when they weren't expecting you and left you in control instead of them.

"Hi, I'm Jeff McReynolds," he said as he walked through the door and stuck out his hand.

"Jack Hodge," the colonel said taking his hand. "What can I do for you?"

"Just a courtesy visit," Jeff said. "Don't know if you have been told or not, but I'm here at the request of the pentagon just to have a little look-see around. Nothing official, but since I was passing through this area on another matter they asked me to stop in and have a look around."

"Anything in particular you are looking for?"

"No, I just wanted to make you aware that I was in the area. Didn't want to be snooping around behind your back. I'll let you know if I need anything." And Jeff got up to leave.

"You do that," Hodge said and offered him his hand. Jeff shook his hand and left, smiling again at the secretary on his way out. Hodge followed Jeff out of the office and after he left he asked Preston. "Who was that man?"

"I don't know. He just walked in and asked if he could see you. What did he tell you?"

"He said he was with the state department. He didn't say it in so many words, but he is here on some kind of fact finding trip. Find out who he is and what he is after?"

"Yes sir," Preston said and as an afterthought added, "Do you think he might be CID?"

"If he is, he's not like any CID man I've ever had experience with."

"I thought he was rather cute," Helga said.

That went rather well Jeff thought to himself as he walked down the hall. Later that evening as he was eating dinner in the hospital mess hall he started thinking again how his first day on the job had gone. His first thought was that this wasn't like any army mess hall he had ever been in. It was more like a large dining room or restaurant. He had taken a seat near the back wall where he could watch the GI's coming in and he wondered if any of them might be the two he was supposed to look for. While walking back up the hill to his room after dinner he started thinking of other assignments he had been on and decided this one might not turn out so terrible after all.

Jeff had been sitting there in the EM Club taking an occasional sip from a whisky sour for almost an hour. The two men had come in not too long after he had and taken a seat three tables away from him. He had been watching them ever since. Finally, he decided they had to be Sergeant Morelocke and Specialists Shipley.

"Pardon me," he said as he approached their table. "I'm looking for a Claude Morelocke and Frank Shipley. Would either of you gentlemen know these men?"

"Maybe," Claude said. "Who's doing the looking?"

"I'm Jeff McReynolds just over from the states and a friend of theirs asked me to look them up."

"Who might this friend be?" Frank asked.

"Harold Sobel."

"Who's Harold Sobel?" Claude asked.

Jeff then realized they probably didn't know about the CIA's presence here and he would have to use a different approach.

"Sorry," Jeff said. "I guess I made a mistake." And he started to walk away.

"Wait," Claude said. "Would you happen to be the gentleman from the state department?"

"Yes."

"Please sit down. We might have something in common after all."

That took Jeff by surprise, but he decided to play along. After all, if these were the two agents Harold had said they were OK, and he sat down with them.

"You have the advantage," he said. "I told you my name, but I still don't know yours."

"I'm Morelocke, and this other handsome young devil here is Shipley," Claude said. "Who is this Harold Sobel and what can we do for you?"

"He's my boss," Jeff said. "Let's cut to the chafe. I know that you are CID and are working a case to find a spy or spies here in Neubrücke. I'm a CIA agent and have been sent over here to work on the case with you."

"How do we know that you are not an imposter, or maybe the spy?"

"You don't. How do I know you are who you say you are?"

"Is this what they call a Mexican standoff?" Frank said, and they all laughed. That Mexican standoff comment and Jeffs answer about Mexican Jumping Beans were codes the agencies used to verify agents legitimacy.

"Now that we have that out of the way let's get to know one another," Claude said, and he told the bar hop to bring them another drink.

For the next two hours the three men sat there talking. Jeff explained who Harold was and how he had become involved. He told them that Harold had suggested they might want to work together, and that is why he had looked them up.

"Would that be a problem for you?" he asked.

"Not for us," Claude said. "But it sure might put a monkey wrench into Major Bradley's plans."

"Harold told me about the major," Jeff said. "What's this about his plans?"

"He likes to think he's the one in charge and probably sees this as an opportunity for glory and a promotion."

"I'll try not to get in his way," Jeff said.

Claude and Frank filled Jeff in on all that had been going on and told him all they knew about what was happening at the hospital. When the bar hop came by and told them it was closing time and asked if they wanted one for the road, they all looked at their watches. The men couldn't believe they had been sitting there talking for so long, but they all agreed it had been a good start.

"Nothing else for me," Jeff said

"Nothing else for us either," Claude said and they all got up to leave.

"Before we go," Jeff said. "Who's the tall red head that works in Hodge's office?"

"That's Helga Detweiler, why?" Claude asked.

"She seems interesting."

"Forget it Jeff. Half the GI's here have been trying to date her ever since she came here. She won't have anything to do with any of them."

"We don't think she's a lesbian," Frank added. "She's just not interested. In fact, she hates our guts."

"I've found that when that's the case there's usually a good reason," Jeff said. "How do you know she's not a lesbian?"

"It's a small hospital," Frank said, "And, word gets around."

"If you're thinking what I think you're thinking, good luck," Claude said.

Two weeks later Claude and Frank about dropped their drinks when Jeff and Helga walked into the EM Club. They were even more surprised when they came over and Jeff asked if they could sit down with them.

"Sure," Claude said as both he and Frank got up.

"Please sit back down," Helga said, "and close your mouths." Later that evening when Jeff and Helga were in his room at the BOQ, "You speak very good English," he told her.

"I was born in England and lived there until I was twelve years old," Helga said. "My father was a diplomat at the German Embassy in London. My mother was a clerk there. They dated for almost a year before getting married, and eight months later I was born. After we had moved back to Berlin I came back to England several times before the war started to visit relatives."

Jeff had never experienced a woman like Helga. She used her body in ways to satisfy him he couldn't have imagined. Afterward, as they were laying there still caressing each other, he told her how satisfying it had been.

"I enjoyed it too," she said.

"Did you live in Berlin during the war?" he asked.

"My father did, but he had sent mother and I away before the city was bombed. He said we would be much safer living somewhere in a small town or village. We found out later he was killed during one of the early bombing raids." Jeff didn't tell her that he had been a bomber pilot and was glad she didn't ask.

"Where did you and your mother live?"

"We lived in Kaiserslautern. Father had a sister that lived there."

Kaiserslautern is the capital city of the Palatinate, one of the six provinces of the Rhineland-Palatinate (Platz.) The German Emperor Fredirich Barbarossa gave the city its name in the 12th century; Kaisers – referring to the emperor, and Lautern – referring to the stream, Lauter, which once ran through the city. It is now an underground river. Kaiserslautern is one of the most important industrial towns in the Platz, largely because of its favorable location at the entrance to the Black Forest. A road existing since pre-Roman times connects the eastern Celtic area with the Rhine River. The Romans once used the road as one of their main supply lines. The town dates back to 1152 when Barbarossa built a magnificent palace there. In 1357, the free imperial city of Kaiserslautern became subject to the Platz. The French, under Napoleon, seized it in 1801. Bavaria took it in 1816, and it was returned to the Palatinate in 1849. It became one of the early stations of Martin Luther's Reformation and became the center of the revolutionary spirit in the Platz. Kaiserslautern's industries consist of spinning and weaving, structural steel, car wheels, boilers, engines, sewing machines, furniture and bricks. In and around Kaiserslautern are extensive quarries of fine stone and forests that supply building and cabinet lumber.

The Platz is often referred to as the quiet section of Germany. It is an area in the southwest corner of Germany with the Rhine River as a border to the east and France on the western border. It is a little known area, mainly rural, unspoiled, and yet with a reliable and serviceable infrastructure. It is the ideal place for enjoying the pleasant German countryside, good food, wine and large stretches of woodlands.

It was a couple of days before Jeff saw Claude and Frank again and they couldn't wait to hear what happened.

"What do you think happened?" Jeff said.

"We can only imagine."

"Among other things, I found out why she hates Americans. Not Americans in general, but just GI's. One night she and her Mom were in a gasthaus near their home when a gang of drunken soldiers came in. They were loud, rude, vulgar, and started verbally abusing the women. Helga and her Mom got up and left, but some of the soldiers followed them out. The men continued to make vulgar remarks to them while following them home. They then forced their way into their home and raped her and her mother. When she told the American authorities about it they laughed at her. The army CID investigator told her that she must have done something to lure the soldiers. Ever since then she has hated the American army and swears she will do whatever it takes to get even with them. That's why she took the job here, and although she didn't say so I got the feeling she is already getting her revenge."

"Why you?" Frank asked.

"What do you mean? Why not me?"

"Like we told you, half the base has been itching to get in her pants and she wouldn't give any of them the time of day. Then you come along and she can't wait to hop in bed with you."

"I don't know, but she sure knew what she was doing."

"Yeah, maybe too well," Claude said. "She has access to every piece of paper that crosses Hodge's desk."

"I hadn't thought of that. Maybe I am being used. However, she made it so enjoyable I didn't even mind."

"What happens now?" Claude asked.

"I don't know, but I hope she continues to use me like that. By the way, I need a car."

"Use mine. Do you have a drivers license?"

"Yes, there was one in the stack of papers Harold gave me."

"Like I said, use my car anytime you want to, but I thought you had a driver?"

"I do, but there will be times I don't want him around."

"I understand," Claude said and handed him one of the extra keys he had.

"Do you think she might be the spy we are looking for?" Frank asked.

"No I don't. Whatever she is doing, she is doing it strictly for revenge.

However, now that you brought it up we do need to find out if she is doing something and who is receiving any information she may be passing on."

There were about a dozen other questions Frank wanted to ask, but the look Jeff gave him said to forget it, I've already told you more than I should have. Frank could tell Jeff was thinking that gentlemen don't kiss and tell. They had gotten all the information about what went on up there in that room that night they were going to get.

"You never told us how your meeting with Hodge went," Frank said.

"OK, I guess. I got the feeling he was trying to figure out if I was the CID agent he had been hearing about. I did hear some interesting talk as I was nosing around in the hospital later that day though."

"Like what?" Claude asked.

"Like someone has started a rumor about there really is a CID man here, and he is here to investigate Hodge."

"I wonder who could have started a rumor like that," Frank said.

"Yeah, I wonder," Jeff said. "I don't think I ever want to piss you two off. I've been hearing some talk about crystals for the MP's radios also."

"You've been picking up too many rumors," Claude said.

"I think you two better lay low for a while. Hodge is taking names and kicking ass. If he finds out you were the ones that started those rumors, or heaven forbid he should find out you are CID or had anything to do with those radios. Well, I think you understand what I am talking about."

"Now about another matter," Jeff said. "How much do you really know about Major Bradley?"

"What do you mean?" Frank asked.

"Hear me out," Jeff said. "Harold had some folks do a background check on him and the results don't look so good."

"Jeff, you know we can't talk about our boss, but let's just say we don't trust him," Claude said.

"OK, suppose I tell you what we've learned then."

"I don't know if we should. The army sort of looks down on trashing ones superior officer."

"You're not the ones doing the trashing. Besides, I get the feeling you already know most of this stuff and don't know what to do with it."

"I guess it won't do no harm to listen," Frank said.

"The short version is that he is incompetent, arrogant and will do anything, including lying and blackmail to get what he wants. He was involved in all that communists in the army mess in Korea, and then lied to Captain Worley about it. Two years ago he almost ruined Sergeant Smith's military career during a case he was working at Fort Sill. He bungled that case so bad the real crook got away clean, and he lied to Smith about that. Since being here, he's led everyone to believe that he is the one in charge and that it is his agents in East Germany. As far as he's concerned the CIA doesn't exist. But, here's the kicker, no one seems to know how he continues to hang around with all that baggage. However, he and General Johnson go back a ways. Something happened while they were both in Korea. Maybe something that Johnson was doing that Bradley apparently found out about. Anyway, they've been thicker than thieves ever since. Several folks have tried to get rid of Bradley, but Johnson dismisses any negative stuff that comes through on him. For example, he was about to be canned for that stunt he pulled at Fort Sill, but Johnson had him transferred over here to his command. If it hadn't been for Johnson, Bradley would never have been assigned to this investigation. The CID was never supposed to have been involved, but Johnson intervened so his buddy Bradley could take charge of the investigation."

"Yeah, we heard most of that stuff," Claude said. "However, like the army manual says, while we may not respect the person we have to respect the uniform and the rank, and he is our superior officer."

"We don't see him any more than we have to," Frank said. "And, when we do we only give him what he asks for. When the time comes to close in on these spies we hope he isn't anywhere around."

"Harold told me to watch out for you two. You're much smarter and have more going on that most folks give you credit for. I'm glad I threw in with you. I'm meeting with Major Bradley tomorrow. Any advice?"

"Keep your hands on your billfold and watch your back."

John R. Bradley grew up in Camden, New Jersey during the depression years. Watching what went on in his lower middle class neighborhood and what his father had to do in order to put food on their table during those depression years shaped the man he would later become. He graduated 124th out of 125 in the 1939 West Point graduating class. The new 2nd Lieutenant's first assignment was as a platoon leader in the 24th Infantry Division at Schofield Barracks in Hawaii. When the Japanese bombed Schofield that Sunday morning on December 7, Lt. Bradley was one of the first officers to rally his men and form a defensive perimeter around the base. That would be the extent of his bravery during the war. After providing the defense for the island of Oahu for several weeks after the attack, the division was sent to Australia to prepare for the American island hopping war that was to come. They were part of the assault forces at New Guinea and later on as part of the assault forces at Leyte when MacArthur made his return to the Philippines. After serving in five campaigns the division left the Philippines for occupation duty in Japan.

Although Lt. Bradley served with honor during his combat experience his performance was less than outstanding. While he was with the occupation forces in Japan he became despondent over not being promoted and made a company commander. He became even more disillusioned with the army when the division became undermanned and ill equipped due to a post war drawdown and reduced military spending. After several run-ins with the MP's for drunk and disorderly conduct he received a reprimand and barely missed receiving a court martial for behavior unbecoming an officer. As a result he asked for and received a transfer to a stateside unit. A series of uneventful assignments followed. After watching a couple of agents track down and convict a GI for robbery he became interested in becoming an army cop and applied for CID school. It was the first thing in his military career he had ever excelled at. He graduated with honors the day Senator Joe McCarthy made his famous speech about Communist in the army. He became a McCarthy disciple, was promoted to captain, and sent to Korea to expose "Reds" serving with the United Nations forces there.

He took this duty serious and began using any means at his disposal to make a name for himself, including badgering, bribery and blackmail. All methods he had learned while watching how the gangs and Mafia families operated during those depression years back there in New Jersey. His methods resulted in having several good and innocent officers removed from active duty, and earned him a reputation as being devious, conniving, and one of the most disrespectful officers one would ever want to come into contact with. Later, while serving with his old outfit, the 24th Division, as an observer and the CID unit commander he caught some of the division general officers committing sins far worse than anything he might have done as unbecoming an officer. He offered to look the other way in return for some favors. He was promoted to Major, and General Johnson never forgot what Bradley did for him.

So far as Bradley was concerned Jeff was from the state department on a fact finding trip. Jeff intended to keep it that way. Their meeting was like two boxers sparing, each punching and jabbing, looking for an opening.

"Look," Jeff finally said. "I know who you are, and about the spies you are looking for. I had a good briefing before coming over here. I'm not here to get involved in your business. The only reason I came to see you is to let you know I am here, and will be in the hospital asking some questions. A senator asked me to do some snooping around. I'll do my best to stay out of your way while I am here."

"Thanks for coming by," Bradley said. "I heard someone had been asking questions and wondered what was going on. Thanks for letting me know."

"Now that we have that out of the way," Jeff said. "There is something you can do for me."

"Just name it," Bradley said.

"I was assigned a driver. His name is Joe Collins. I don't trust him. Would it be possible for you to do some checking up on him for me?"

"I think that might be something I could do."

"Thanks," Jeff said and he shook Bradley's hand and left.

"Peculiar," Jeff said to Joe as he got back in the car.

"What's that?" Joe asked.

"Bradley. He was asking about my driver. Wanted to know who he was and if he was from around here."

Later that evening at the O Club Jeff chuckled to himself as he thought about what he had done. Harold would be proud, and as he looked up from his drink Harold walked through the door.

"To what do I owe this honor," Jeff said as Harold pulled up a chair and sat down.

"Just came by to see how things were going."

"Well now, let's see, I've made contact with the two CID agents, and they are every bit as talented as you said they were. I've also had my meetings with Colonel Hodge and Major Bradley, and I got laid by Colonel Hodge's secretary."

"As a matter of business I assume."

"No sir. That was strictly pleasure."

"Sounds like you've had a very busy few weeks. Now buy me a drink and give me the long version."

Jeff ordered a drink for Harold and another one for himself and told Harold all that had been going on. He also told him that he didn't trust his driver and how he had set it up so that Bradley and Joe would be spying on each other, and how he thought the German girl he had gone to bed with might be working against the Americans and why she had a reason to.

"What have Claude and Frank been able to find out about the reports?" Harold asked.

"Nothing concrete yet, but I get the feeling they may know more than they have told me."

"And, you don't think that this Helga, Hodges secretary has anything to do with it?"

"Not with any of that other stuff, but I think she may be doing something."

"Besides taking CIA spooks to bed?"

"Well that too, but she has a motive and she has the opportunity to see some very sensitive information. She gave in much too easy to me. Claude said that half the base had been trying to date her and she wouldn't give them the time of day."

"And you plan to keep seeing her?"

"Every chance I get."

"I don't have to tell you to be careful, but I will anyway. You watch your back."

"What aren't you telling me, Harold?" Jeff asked.

"I don't understand. What do you mean?"

"How are the reports or messages from the hospital being sent over to East Germany?"

"By radio, why?"

"That's what I'm talking about. We're being played. They are only letting us hear what they want us to hear. If it was anything important they wouldn't be broadcasting it, they would be using a courier. All those reports are just eyewash. That's not what this is all about."

Harold smiled and said, "Just wanted to see if you would come to the same conclusion. I didn't want to prejudice your thinking. I think that is exactly what is going on. How did you come to that conclusion?"

"I've been over that hospital with a fine tooth comb and don't see anything or any reason for what's going on. I'm sure that Claude came to that same conclusion also long before Frank ever got here. Whatever it is, it's happening for a reason, but it's not about that hospital. What happens now?"

"We still need to find out why it's happening and who is responsible. That's why I ask you if you were sure that it wasn't Helga. What makes you think Claude might have come to the same conclusion?"

"Just from my conversations with them. Neither he nor Frank think there is a good reason for them being here."

"We've still got a job to do," Harold said. "And until we know what or who we are dealing with here I don't trust anyone, so like I said, you be careful." And, with that he got up and left.

"Well, what have you found out?" Hodge asked.

"I think it's only rumors. I'm trying to run down the source of a couple of them now. However, I did confirm there was a CID officer doing some snooping around," Stovall told him.

"Is it that McReynolds guy?"

"No, he's legitimate. I did some checking on him. He really is from the state department. Some GI complained to his senator about the treatment he received while he was a patient here. That senator who just happens to be up for reelection sent McReynolds over here to check up on us."

"So you think it's nothing more than just some rumors about a CID investigation?"

"So far as I've been able to find out that's what's going on. I'll know more about it after I check out the source of those rumors."

"You let me know as soon as you find out."

"You'll be the first to know sir," and Stovall saluted and walked out.

"I hope you had some good news for him." Sergeant Preston said to him when he came out of the colonel's office.

"Only time will tell," Stovall told him. Major Stovall wasn't about to tell either Hodge or Preston what he actually thought. There was a whole lot more going on in Hodge's command right now than met the eye. Some of it might even be going on in Hodge's office. What was Helga all about? Her hooking up with Jeff so fast. Half the men here had been wanting to get in her pants and she was like an ice berg. But, as soon as Jeff walks in she's hot to trot. Yes sir, a lot more going on than Hodge and Preston needed to know about just yet.

SIX

THE SPY

F rank Shipley grew up in the mountains of East Tennessee listening to the
stories the sheriff's deputies told while they ate bologna sandwiches for
lunch at the little store where he worked during high school. After graduating
from college with a degree in Criminal Justice he went to work for the county
sheriff's office. Frank liked to brag that he was the chief of detectives, but
the truth was, he was the only detective the sheriff had. The biggest criminal
problem the county had was the occasional moonshine still. That is until the
year the carnival came through for the Fourth of July holiday and the body
showed up when they left town. For as long as anyone could remember the
carnival always showed up for the Fourth of July and always set up on the
county fairgrounds. It was the highlight of the year. It was the perfect place
to take your girl for the evening and Frank always hoped the Ferris Wheel
would get stuck while they were way up there on top, but it never did. The
carnival wasn't as much fun after he went to work for the sheriff's office and
was always on duty that week. Walking around watching for pickpockets or
kids trying to sneak into the hoochie coochie show wasn't as much fun as
trying to sneak a feel or steal a kiss while in the Tunnel of Love.

After working long hours during carnival week he had taken a few days off
and was at the river fishing when the sheriff sent the deputy to find him.
On the way back to the court house the deputy filled him in on what was
going on. While some of the inmates were cleaning up after the carnival left
town they found a body in one of the dumpsters. His empty wallet was also
in the dumpster. All the money was missing but the identification was still
in it. Just to make sure Frank had sent his fingerprints off to Washington.

The ID in the wallet found with the man identified him as George Cole from Rome, Georgia. Instead of receiving a report from Washington, an FBI agent showed up in the little mountain town to see Frank. George Cole had been drafted into the army, but failed to show up for his induction. That was more than ten months ago, and the FBI and CID had been looking for him ever since. When the fingerprints showed up at their crime lab it was the first clue they had about his whereabouts. It seemed to Frank the FBI man was far more interested in making sure the body was that of George Cole than he was in finding out what had happened to him. He wasn't too impressed with the government agent, but hadn't expected much more after watching how some of their T Men investigated moonshine still reports.

While George might not have been from East Tennessee, and considered an army deserter, the crime had been committed in his county and Frank considered it his case to solve. The next day he drove across the mountains to Greenville, South Carolina. The Carnival owner had some questions to answer. Yes, George had been working for the carnival, but he hadn't seen him for a couple of days. Although this was the first real crime Frank had ever investigated he knew from the way Sam, the carnival owner, acted and talked he knew more than he was telling.

"We can do this any one of three different ways," Frank told Sam. "Either you start being honest with me and give me all the information I want, or two, I will have the Greenville police shut you down, place you under arrest, and haul your ass back across the mountain to answer some questions about something that happened while your carnival was in our county, or three, since George was an army deserter I will call in the FBI and let you deal with them." Frank's sudden toughness shocked Sam. This green kid didn't look like he had that in him.

"I didn't know George was an army deserter," Sam said. "He had only been with us for a few months. He was a good worker and had started relieving some of the operators on the rides when they took a break. In order to relax after a long days work some of us get together to have a little drink and play some poker after we shut the carnival down for the night. Sometimes the game lasts all night and we grab a few hours sleep before opening up the next day. Some of the boys noticed that George always seemed to win and thought he might be cheating. They set a little trap for him and that last night up there in Tennessee caught George cheating. I told him that I couldn't have someone I didn't trust working for me and for him to get out. That's the last time I saw him."

"Well, someone at that poker game saw him after that. He was found dead in one of our dumpsters while we were cleaning up the grounds after you left. I want to see all the men that were in that card game."

"It may take a while to round all of them up."

"I'm not going anywhere."

After all the men had been brought in Frank explained to them what was going on. He realized the chance he was taking that whoever was responsible would not run off. But, what none of them realized was that he had a long conversation with the Greenville police chief before ever coming out to the carnival site. The chief had agreed to provide whatever aid and assistance he wanted. Several police officers and two plain close detectives were already on the job watching Frank's back while he was talking to the carnival workers. In less than an hour after Frank left the meeting two of the men had been picked up by the Greenville police when they tried to leave the carnival grounds.

As the army began to ramp up for WW II the crime rate had also risen with the expansion of personnel. To cope with this the Criminal Investigation Division of the army that was first established during WW I by General Pershing was ramped up along with it. The CID had been set up initially to prevent and detect crime among the American Expeditionary Force in France. At the end of that war the US Army was reduced in size during the transition to peacetime and the size of the CID was reduced accordingly. With the onset of WW II the army once again became a force of millions and the need for a self-policing law enforcement system was needed once again. The organization exercises supervision over criminal investigation activities, coordinates investigations between commands, dictates plans and policies and sets standards for criminal investigations. Military Special Agents receive training as Military Policemen and after graduation from MP school receive further training as CID agents.

Shortly after going to work for the sheriff's office Frank had joined the local Army National Guard unit, and had become their acting Provost Marshal. He had volunteered for the active duty assignment and because of his National Guard training had been sent to the MP School at Fort Gordon, Georgia. After graduating from the CID school at Fort Gordon SP5 Shipley was assigned as a special agent to the artillery school at Fort Sill, Oklahoma. Sergeant Claude Morelocke had been one of his instructors at Fort Gordon. Shortly after Frank had graduated from CID school sergeant Morelocke had been given a special assignment at the 98th Hospital in Germany. When Lt Stevens was poisoned, Specialists Shipley had been sent to the 6th CC as his replacement.

Frank didn't know why, but the information he had in his shirt pocket and what was about to happen had caused him to remember how alone and vulnerable he had felt in that room with all those carnival workers so long ago. He had been sitting there thinking about that and toying with his beer for more than an hour when Claude finally asked him what was wrong.

"What do you mean?" Frank asked.

"You haven't exactly been the life of the party this evening. What's going on?"

"I guess I have been a little distracted."

"A little distracted. You have been sitting there running your finger around the top of your glass and haven't said a word for the last ten minutes. You didn't even notice a minute ago when that girl tried to flirt with you."

"Something's bothering me."

"That's obvious. Is it something you care to share?"

"How much do you know about these little trips Lyons takes?"

"I told you all I know about that, why?" Frank reached in his shirt pocket and took out a folded paper, unfolded it and slid it across the table to Claude. "Jeff brought that by the message center this afternoon." He said.

"So."

"Look at it. Lyons went missing the day before yesterday, and yesterday that showed up in East Germany."

"What are you trying to say?"

"After Jeff dropped that off I got to thinking. I went back and pulled out all the reports I have and then tried to remember what the dates were that Lyons went missing. As near as I can remember, every time he goes on one of his little drunks is when one of those messages is sent over to the bad guys."

"I can't believe what I'm hearing." Claude said. "Are you insinuating that Lyons is a spy?"

"I hate to say it, but I believe he is."

"Have you told anyone else about this?"

"No one. I just figured it out this afternoon."

"Are you going to tell Bradley?"

"Absolutely not. He's the last person I want to know about this."

"What are you going to do?"

"One of us needs to follow Lyons the next time he decides to take off."

"We can't do that. He would spot one of us a mile off."

"There's more," Frank said.

"What now?" Claude asked. Frank reached in his shirt pocket again and slid another piece of paper across to Claude.

"That's another list of messages that have been sent to the Stasi."

"What's the difference?"

"There is no way Lyons could have known that information. Someone else is also giving information to the East Germans, and I think I know who that someone is."

"Who?"

"Helga."

"How do you know that?"

"Because most of that stuff would have come from Colonel Hodge's office."

"My God, are you suggesting that the Colonel is involved?"

"No. What I'm suggesting is that Jeff may have gotten involved in more than he knows right now."

"Have you talked to him about this yet?"

"No. Like I told you, I only figured this out this afternoon."

"We need to see Jeff first thing in the morning," Claude said.

While Claude and Frank were sitting in Höhns worrying about what to do with the information Frank had uncovered Jeff was sitting in the O Club trying to figure out what was going on. What had been happening with him just didn't feel right. Claude had told him that Helga was an ice berg, but she had practically thrown herself in bed with him. Harold had suggested that she might be a distraction. If that were the case, a distraction from what? He felt he was being used and had told Harold so. He had been through something almost exactly like this on one of his first assignments. While he was working as an oil rigger in Saudi Arabia several years ago, a young Arab woman had come on to him when it was strictly taboo for an Arab woman to even be seen with an infidel much less to speak with one. While she was entertaining him, the saboteur he had been sent to find had almost succeeded in setting fire to the oil field. He wasn't about to make that same mistake again with Helga, no matter how much fun it was being with her.

As Jeff was sitting down to breakfast the next morning Frank and Claude came over to his table and said, "We need to talk."

"And a good morning to you too. What has you two so wound up this early in the morning?"

"We've identified the spy." Claude said.

"The hell you say."

"Remember all those reports I asked you to get for me?" Frank asked.

"Yes."

"Well, in going through them and timing when sergeant Lyons was on one of his little trips it looks like every time he goes away one of those reports shows up in East Germany."

"You think Lyons is the spy?"

"It saddens us to say so, but it looks like it," Claude said.

"But you don't have any proof?"

"Someone is going to have to follow him the next time he takes off in order to get the proof," Frank said.

"And I'm elected. Is that what you are trying to tell me?"

"It can't be one of us. He would spot us a mile away. Besides, neither of us can afford to be AWOL like Paul does," Claude said.

"Here's the way we figure it," Frank said. "The next time he takes off we will notify you and you do the follow act."

"How do I manage that since I don't have a car and couldn't get my driver here in time?"

"You have the keys to my car," Claude said.

"But won't he spot that?"

"That's a chance we have to take. Chances are if he does see it and doesn't see me or Frank around he will just think it's another car like mine and won't pay any attention."

They didn't have to wait long. It was only a couple of days later Paul got up and started putting on his class A uniform. Claude engaged Paul in a lengthy conversation about some bogus hospital issue while Frank hurried downstairs to the orderly room and placed a call to Jeff. Paul was already gone when Jeff arrived and they were afraid they had missed him. However, as Jeff was going out the gate he saw Paul getting in a cab in front of the bahnhof.

It was three days before Jeff returned, and by then both Claude and Frank were getting worried. They had made plans that if Jeff didn't return by tonight they would go see Harold. They were sitting in the EM Club when Jeff walked it.

"We were getting worried about you," they said.

"It's a long story fellas, and I'm thirsty," Jeff said. After ordering a beer and taking a long drink, Jeff began to tell his story. "I followed him to a gasthaus in Ruckweiler. I watched him go in and then went in myself. We were the only two people in there. After taking only a few sips of my beer I got up and left because I thought my being there with him or them alone might spook him. I went back out to the car and watched. When after a few minutes several more folks started showing up I went back in and took a table as far away from Paul as I could and ordered another beer. After about thirty minutes a gentleman came in, and after looking around he went over and sat down with Paul. I couldn't hear what they were saying, but the other man was writing. Paul never gave him a note or anything, only talked, and all the while the other man wrote down most of what he said. I don't know what happened to Paul because I went back out to the car and waited for the other man to leave. When he did I followed him to an office building in Kaiserslautern. Or at least I thought it was an office building, but it must have been some sort of a combination office-apartment complex because he never came back out. I watched it for two days, then came back here."

"What happens now?" Claude asked.

"I think we need to have Major Stovall take Sergeant Lyons into custody."

"Why Stovall?"

"Do either one of you want to arrest him?"

"I don't think so," Claude said.

"What about Bradley?" Jeff asked.

"We don't want him involved," Frank said.

"I hope you know what you are doing," Jeff said.

"We'll tell him it was your doing," Claude said.

"Thanks a lot. Is Lyons here now?"

"He came in this morning."

"Then I guess this is as good a time as any. Let's go get Stovall."

Paul was lying on his bunk dressed in his underwear reading a magazine when Stovall walked in.

"Sergeant Lyons?"

"Yes."

"You need to get dressed and come with me."

"Why?"

"You've been taking a lot of unauthorized trips lately and some folks want to talk to you about them."

"Am I under arrest?"

"I hope that won't be necessary."

Stovall hadn't been told the whole story, but when Jeff had come to him he guessed what was going on. He hoped Lyons wouldn't make a big deal out of it. He didn't want to have to put him under arrest. Out of all the people he had met here he liked Lyons as much or more than any of them. Lyons had always been courteous and friendly to his MP's and even saw to it they received snacks and coffee while they were on patrol. He hoped Jeff was wrong about Paul. He had Helga pegged as the spy. Stovall took Lyons to his office where Jeff was waiting for him. They had decided that it would be better if Lyons didn't know that Frank and Claude were involved. They didn't show up until after Sergeant Lyons had been brought in and was in Stovall's office. They were waiting in the outer office in case they were needed.

"What the hell is he doing here?" Frank said. His remark startled Claude and he looked up just in time to see Major Bradley coming through the door.

"Were you planning on inviting me to the party?" Bradley said as he walked past them.

"It's hardly a party Major," Claude said. "Paul is a good friend, and he is not a traitor."

"We'll see about that. I'll take charge now," Bradley said.

"Shit!" Both Frank and Claude said at the same time under their breath.

Jeff came out of Stovall's office just as Bradley said he was in charge. Bradley glared at him and without saying anything went in the office. Frank and Claude started to get up, but Jeff motioned for them to sit back down.

"I handle this," he said and went back in the office.

By the time he got back in the office Bradley was already questioning Lyons. Stovall was sitting off to the side.

"Why Sergeant Lyons?" Bradley asked.

"My wife," Lyons answered.

"Your wife?"

"Yes. You see sir I was in what is now East Germany when the war ended. I fell in love with a German girl and married her. When that part of Germany became the Russian Zone after the war our unit, along with all the others, was sent back over here and eventually back to the states. I tried to stay in Germany, but the army wouldn't let me. They also didn't approve of the marriage, so I couldn't take Gisela with me. After I left she went back to East Germany to live with her parents. I started to get out of the army and come back over here. But, after talking to a congressman he convinced me that it would be useless for me to try and get into East Germany and get her out. So I decided to stay in the army and transfer to another unit that was being deployed back over here. I was able to visit her a few times, but the Russians finally closed the border and wouldn't let me in or her out. I tried everything I knew to keep in touch with her and did manage to get a few messages through and got one or two replies back from her. Then one day a man came to see me. He had pictures of Gisela and her parents and told me if I ever wanted to see her alive again I would do what he asked me to. Ever since then I have been giving them what information they want."

"How do you communicate with them?"

"By notes. Someone at the commissary gives me a note while I am there buying food for the hospital. The note has instructions telling me where and when to meet him."

"Who at the commissary gives you these notes?"

"I don't know. It could be anybody. The note is usually with my shopping list when I get it back."

"How about the gentleman you meet with, is it always the same man?"

"Yes, and all I know about him is that he told me to call him George when we talk. He tells me what information they are looking for and when and where the next meeting will take place. I've tried to be as careful as I could. I try to give them as little information as I can when answering their questions. I didn't want to do anything that would hurt this unit or the army, but at the same time I didn't want them to hurt Gisela either."

"Are you willing to work with us so we can learn who these people are and what all is involved here?"

"No sir, not if it will put Gisela in danger."

"I promise you no harm will come to her, and I will do everything in my power to not only see that she remains safe, but to get her out of East Germany as well. In addition, I will do all I can to see that none of this ever goes in your records and that when the time comes you can retire honorably."

Jeff had been sitting there listening to Bradley and finally had all he could stand. He got up and walked to the center of the office just in front of where Lyons was sitting. He looked at Bradley then turned to Lyons and told him to go get a cup of coffee.

"What are you doing?" Bradley asked.

"Trying to keep you from telling any more lies. I'll not sit here quietly any longer and be a part of your deception. You just made a bunch of promises you have no way, and probably had no intention of keeping."

"You have no right to interfere with my investigation. I was the one that found out what was going on and I'll be the one to see this thing through."

"No. Your two agents were the ones to realize what was happening and managed to solve this mystery in spite of you. Now you're trying to take credit not only for what they did, but for my doing all the leg work as well.

You lied to Worley about being in Korea and the mess your agents made there. You almost ruined Smith's career, and then lied to him about your involvement in that mess in Oklahoma in order to get his cooperation. You took all the credit for breaking up that drug cartel when you actually had very little to do with it. Now you are about to ruin another man's career and maybe get his wife killed in the process. You are some piece of work Major. You're a disgrace to your country and to the uniform you wear. You're through here. Now get the hell out of here and out of my investigation."

"You can't talk to me that way," Bradley said. "And, you have no right interfering with my interrogation."

"I can talk to you any way I want to," Jeff said. "And, I have every right to not only interfere with your so called interrogation, but to take charge of it as well. I am a CIA special agent. I was sent here by the director to get to the bottom of this so called spy business. I intend to do just that in spite of your incompetence and lies. Major Stovall, get this lying piece of shit out of here and have some of your men escort him off of the base." Major Stovall was stunned, but soon recovered and took Bradley by the elbow and guided him out of the room. "Sergeant Harrell, take this man to his vehicle and see that he leaves the base."

"Yes sir," Harrell said and escorted the major out. After Bradley had been removed, Jeff had Sergeant Lyons brought back in the room.

"I'm sorry Bradley told you all that stuff," Jeff said. "He had no right making you all those promises. He has no way of finding Gisela for you or of keeping her safe, much less of getting her out of East Germany."

"Who are you?" Lyons asked.

"I'm Jeff McReynolds, and I work for the state department."

"Another spook," Lyons said.

"Maybe, but we're not all like Bradley."

"Why should I listen to or believe anything any of you people say?"

"I don't blame you, but before you throw all this away please listen to what I have to offer before you decide that all of us are bad. If you don't want to go along with us then I'll understand."

"OK, I'll listen. But I'm not saying I'll cooperate with you."

"I was the one that followed you that last time when you met George in Ruckweiler. I followed him to Kaiserslautern after he left you. I don't know if he went anywhere after that. I watched him for two days and he didn't leave his apartment."

"Now I remember you Paul said. I wondered why you only took a sip of your beer and left so fast."

"I was afraid me being there would spook whoever was meeting you since there were only the two of us in there."

"It would have," Paul said. "Once before there wasn't anyone else round when George came in and he wouldn't stay. He had me meet him the next day at another gasthaus."

"I won't promise you that Gisela won't get hurt, but our agents that are already in East Germany will do everything in their power to find her and keep her safe. After that, we will send in another agent who will get to know her and she will then try her best to get Gisela out. I won't promise you that any of this will be successful. However, we will do our best. You see, Sergeant Lyons, we don't know who these people are or why they have been using you. The stuff you have been sending them is of no military use what so ever. That's why we need to find out who they are and what's going on. We might be able to find out what's going on without your help, but it would be a lot easier if you will cooperate with us. Do you mind if I ask you a few more questions?"

"Do I have a choice?"

"Yes, you can get up and leave now. However, if you do the army will place you under arrest for treason and you will be sent to Leavenworth for the rest of your life. Or, you can stay here, answer a few more questions, and help us try and rescue Gisela. If you do I promise we will do everything we can for both you and Gisela."

"I thought you said I had a choice. OK, what are your questions?"

"Did you start taking your little two and three day vacations after George first talked to you?"

"No, I was doing that long before I ever saw George. That's part of the reason I've been busted so many times. I was a battalion mess sergeant in the 278th Armored Infantry Battalion down in Stuttgart. Sometimes I would have a dream or sometimes I would just get to thinking about Gisela and it would about drive me mad, so I would go get drunk for a couple of days. The battalion S1 was an old buddy from our days together during the war, and he kept most of the stuff out of my records. We had a 1st Lt company commander that was a West Point graduate and he was a stickler for rules and regulations. He would take one or two of my stripes every time I got drunk and left home. As soon as I got them back I would go and do it all over again. He found out my buddy was keeping my personnel record clean and had me reassigned up here. He didn't want any screwups in his unit. I'd been up here for several months and had been on several of those unauthorized leaves when I met George. He came up to me one night in a gasthaus and started talking. That's when he showed me that picture of Gisela and her folks and told me if I ever wanted to see them again I would do what he said. If I'd been sober I probably would have clobbered him. He said I would be told what to do and the next time I went to the commissary was when I got the first note."

"That means they had been watching you for a while. They knew your habits and knew no one would notice when you were gone. You go back to your unit and keep cooperating with them. I'll let you know when we need to see you again."

"That's it. I'm free to go?"

"Yes, but I'm going to put a watch on you. Not because I don't trust you. He'll be there to watch your back just in case George gets any ideas and for us to keep an eye on George and see who else is involved. He's not acting alone. If we're lucky he may lead us to whoever is in charge of this operation. I'm sure George saw me while I was following you that day, so we will be changing agents periodically so he doesn't catch on. Just warning you in case you notice different folks following you around. Hopefully you won't see us at all. In the mean time, I'll have one of our agents in East Germany start looking for Gisela. Do you have a picture of her I can give him?"

"I have one, but its several years old."

"I'll take it. It might be helpful, and we will begin the search in that town of what did you call it – Gardelegen?"

"Very good. You say it better than I can. That's where they were living when I met her. I don't know where they are now."

"Don't worry sergeant, we'll find her."

After Lyons left, Major Stovall who had been sitting there quietly all this time got up and walked over to the only window in his office. After standing there looking up the street at the massive hospital complex for several minutes, he slowly turned to Jeff and said, "What else?"

"What do you mean?"

"What happens now?"

"We will do everything in our power to find Gisela and get her out of East Germany."

"I was talking about Sergeant Lyons. What happens to him now?"

"I don't know. I don't plan to bring any charges against him. Yes, I know what he did was potentially treasonous, but none of that stuff he gave them was of any importance to anyone. I can't justify what he did, but I also can't say that I wouldn't have done the same thing if I had been in his shoes. Besides, what he did didn't hurt anyone. I guess it's in the hands of the army what will happen to him now. Personally I hope nothing happens until we bring Gisela out of East Germany and reunite them."

"I'll see to it the army turns its back on what has happened here," Stovall said. "Do you need any help rounding up George, or whatever his name is?"

"No, I think the agency can take care of that. We will watch him for a while to see if anyone else is involved."

"What about here?" Stovall asked.

"What do you mean?"

"Do you think anyone else here was or is involved in any of this?"

What an odd question Jeff thought. How much does he really know?

Gardelegen is a town in Saxony-Anhalt, Germany on the main rail line about half way between Berlin and Hanover. It was first founded in the tenth century and has been almost totally destroyed several times. First by the French during the thirty years war and the last time by the allies during WW II. It is said to produce some of the best beer in the Russian Zone of East Germany. By the start of WW II Gardelegen had become a highly industrialized town producing agricultural machinery. All these factories were converted to the production of aircraft and trucks for the Third Reich. Gisela's Dad, Henrich Krupa had been a machinists in one of these factories. Had it not been for that he would have been conscripted for the army like Gisela's two brothers were. She never saw them again.

In 1945 when allied troops entered Nazi Germany, the SS began evacuating prisoners from concentration camps. Sending them on death marches into the interior of the country. Following the US Army's crossing of the Rhine River the SS administrator at the Dora-Mittelbau Concentration Camp ordered all the prisoners moved to Bergen-Belsen. Within days, some 4000 prisoners arrived in the Gardelegen area. They had to dismount from the freight cars because the trains couldn't go any further due to rail damage caused by air raids. Because the SS guards were greatly outnumber by the prisoners, they began to recruit anyone they could find to help guard the prisoners. Over a thousand of these prisoners were taken to a barn just out of town where they were locked inside, and the barn set on fire. Those trying to escape were shot by the guards. The next day while the SS were trying to dispose of the evidence of their crime, elements of the 102nd Infantry Division entered the town and stopped them. The commander of the US unit that liberated the town ordered the citizens of the town to be rounded up and forced to bury the more than one thousand charred remains the US troops found in the still smoldering barn. Master Sergeant Paul Lyons was a mess sergeant in one of the US battalions that entered Gardelegen.

Gisela had only been fourteen years old when the war started. Although the family had been put on rations like everyone else they had managed a little better because of her father's position at the factory. His turning machine that was making crank shafts for tractor engines before the war was now producing aircraft engine parts. Their picturesque old town had managed to survive without any war damage for more than four years. All that changed one April night in 1944 when the RAF Lancaster bombers came. The next day B 17's from the 8th Bomb Group finished the job. Henrich Krupa escaped with his life but lost one of his legs in the bomb raid. Several houses and their church had also been destroyed. Life for Gisela would never be the same. The once proud Frau Krupa now scavenged in the streets for scraps of anything edible to keep the family from starving. When the troops from the 102nd Division came to town, Gisela began selling her body for something to eat. One night in a gasthaus sergeant Lyons saw her and after a couple of beers took her back to his quarters. That started a new life for Gisela. After that night she was Lyons girl, and since he was a mess sergeant Gisela and her family was no longer starving. Shortly before the Americans left and the Russians took over Louis and Gisela were married. It was a German marriage and never sanction by the army. Paul hadn't bothered to get the army's permission.

SEVEN

OPERATION RESCUE

———————————

B obby Joe Knight, alias Alfred Lowden, was surprised to see an older version of the woman in the picture he had in his shirt pocket walk into the gasthaus. He was sure it was Gisela Lyons, but how was he going to make sure. It didn't seem that any of the handful of others in the gasthaus was interested in Gisela, but he needed to be sure before speaking to her. None of the others had come in with her, and no one else had come in after she came in and sat down at a table in the corner by herself. There was an older couple sitting near the door and they didn't even look up when she walked in. It was obvious what the young couple at the back table was interested in, and it certainly wasn't Gisela. While Alfred was watching the young man slipped his hand under the table and after placing it on her knee, he slowly moved it up her leg. The young lady giggled and then leaned over and kissed him. The only other person in the gasthaus that had shown any interest had started looking up from his beer and glancing over at Gisela. However, the looks he was giving her were more of a wonder what you would be like in bed look. He was no threat and soon looked at his watch and got up to leave. The few others hadn't even bothered to look up. They were much more interested in each other and their beers than in either he or Gisela. Alfred decided to chance it and got up and walked over to Gisela's table. He discretely laid the photograph down on her napkin and said, "I believe this belongs to you," and turned around and walked back over to his table. Before he sat back down, Gisela was already on the way to his table.

"Where did you get this?" she asked as she sat down.

"I got it from a man who got it from Paul."

"That's not possible. They told me he was dead."

"He's very much alive and wanting to see you."

"But, they showed me pictures of a wreck and pictures of Paul and a newspaper article explaining the wreck and those killed in it."

"All fake," Alfred said. "We shouldn't be seen together for long. Two weeks from today a woman will meet you here and explain it all to you and have a plan for getting you back to Paul." Before Gisela could say anything else he got up and left the gasthaus. Gisela sat there stunned. Neither of them noticed the waitress on the phone.

The Stasi, or East German Secret Police was developed out of the internal security and police apparatus established by the soviets after WW II. The Ministry for State Security, or Stasi as it was known was patterned after the Soviet KGB. It soon made Nazism look like a Sunday school picnic. It was a highly effective secret police organization, and it had infiltrated every institution of society and every aspect of daily life. It accomplished this goal through a vast network of informants and unofficial collaborators who spied on and denounced colleagues, friends, neighbors and even family members. In addition to domestic surveillance, the Stasi was also responsible for foreign surveillance and intelligence gathering. At the height of the cold war the Stasi had extensively penetrated West Germany's government and military intelligence services. Although supposedly an independent German organization the KGB maintained liaison officers in all Stasi directorates. The waitress at the gasthaus Gisela often frequented was a Stasi informant. Before Alfred had even started backing his car out of the parking lot that night the Stasi already knew about his and Gisela's meeting.

Irma Heigl was a second generation German-American. Her father Henry Heigl had fled Germany shortly before WW I and went to work as a master brewer at the Joseph Schlitz Brewery in Milwaukee, Wisconsin. Neither Henry nor his wife spoke English. Irma learned to speak English in school.

She was a senior at the University of Wisconsin when the CIA recruiters visited the campus. Setting in an office sorting through and interpreting intercepted messages from East Germany was not what she had in mind when she joined the CIA. She had begged for a field assignment, but every request had been turned down. When she was summoned into Bill's office she had visions of being fired. However, He had something else in mind. After extensive questioning she was told to report to their field training facilities at Langley, Virginia. She was the only female German speaking agent available on such short notice. A normal six month training cycle would have to be condensed into two weeks. Irma proved not only to be highly intelligent, but a quick learner as well. The fire arms training almost proved to be her undoing. She was afraid of guns. With only two days left before the assignment was either a go or called off she finally qualified, but was told to use the weapon only as a last resort.

Irma had been taken out of an office clerks job and put through two weeks of the most grueling training imaginable and still didn't know what for. When the assignment was explained to her she hesitated before agreeing to do the job. Not that she was afraid or concerned for her own safety, but being responsible for the life of someone else was a new concept to her. After hearing that she was the only hope Gisela had of being brought out of East Germany and reunited with her husband in the foreseeable future and maybe ever, she reluctantly agreed. We have given you the best training possible for the job she was told. You will keep your name since the Germans won't have had time to check it out. You will be given a complete work history in the East German State Ministry for Missing Persons in Berlin, and your excuse for going to Gardelegen is to visit the cemetery where those murdered during a massacre near the end of the war are interred. You are looking for information for a family member. You shouldn't have any trouble crossing the border out of Berlin into East Germany, but if you do you are to immediately abort the mission. The field agent that first made contact with Gisela will be with you in Gardelegen and will be watching your back the whole time you are there. He is working on an escape plan. His name is Alfred Lowden. All the information we've just discussed, and all the information we have about Gisela and as much info as we could find about Gardelegen is in a packet you will be given as you board the plane for Berlin. We suggest you study and memorize it on the trip over. Good luck.

Contact made, suggest we meet in Berlin to discuss, was the message Alfred had sent to Jeff. Understood, will be on tomorrow's courier flight to Tempelhof, Jeff radioed back,

"What's going on?" Jeff was asking before they had even sat down.

"You do have a way of getting right to the point, don't you," Alfred said.

"I'm sorry," Jeff said. "I guess I'm just a little stressed out and overly anxious. Order us a beer and let's start over again."

While they were waiting for their beers to arrive Alfred said, "Something's not right."

"What do you mean?"

"Something smells with this program. I was told that Gisela was being held hostage. Nothing could be farther from the truth. It was pure luck that I found her, but she walked into that gasthaus as free as a bird. She didn't hesitate to speak to and talk to me. She had been told that her husband, this sergeant Lyons had been killed in an accident. They had even shown her pictures of the accident and a newspaper article about it complete with Lyons' picture. But, she told me that at no time was she ever threatened or held hostage."

"Wow, that gives it a whole new meaning doesn't it," Jeff said.

"You bet it does. Are you still going through with it?"

"I'll have to think that over."

"Well, while you are thinking here's something else for you to consider. I said she was not being held hostage. That doesn't mean she is not being watched."

"By whom?"

"It could be anyone. The Stasi has spies all over. It could even be someone in her family."

"Is the agent we are sending in going to be in harms way?"

"I can't promise you that she won't be. Is that going to be a problem?"

"It could be a big one. Up until yesterday she was in an office sorting and translating papers. She has never been out in the field."

"How could they even consider sending someone like that over here?"

"It's a have to situation. She is the only German speaking female agent available right now. It's either her or call the whole thing off. Give me some guidance here Alfred. What chance do we have of pulling this off?"

"Based on what you just told me, I'd say less than thirty percent."

"That little, huh? What would you do Alfred?"

"Oh no, you're not putting this off on me. That decision is way above my pay grade."

"It may be above mine too, but I say let's go ahead with what we have. Give her all the help you can. Her name is Irma Heigl."

After the decision had been made, Jeff felt like he had just pronounced a death sentence on both Irma and Gisela. He explained the identity that had been created for Irma and together they outlined a plan of escape. Alfred told Jeff that getting Irma into Germany wouldn't be the problem. Getting both of them out would. Jeff then asked "if it would be easier to get only one of them out?"

"What do you have in mind?" Alfred asked.

"What if only Gisela leaves East Germany?"

"I don't follow you. What happens to Irma?"

"Gisela becomes Irma and goes back to Berlin. Irma and you would go west and leave East Germany somewhere at a little insignificant border crossing."

"That just might work," Alfred said. "But, why should I come back with her?"

"Because after all this is over I suspect that your cover will have been compromised."

"Hell, my cover has probably been compromised a dozen times before."

"That may very well be, but none of those other times involved kidnapping someone they were watching and using right out from under their noses."

"Point well taken."

"I'll leave it up to you and Irma to work out the details when she gets here. Good luck."

Jeff flew back to Frankfurt after his meeting in Berlin with Alfred, and while Claude was driving him back to Neubrücke he explained what was going on.

"I don't understand," Claude said. "You mean that all this stuff with Paul has only been a smoke screen?"

"Looks that way."

"But, why?"

"That's something we're going to have to figure out. When there's a diversion there is usually a reason for it."

"Frank has been doing some more digging while you've been gone and may have some information about that."

"Like what?"

"He's pulled all the reports that have been intercepted since this thing started and has discovered something rather startling."

"Like what?"

"All the information about this region was not sent over to the Stasi by Paul."

"What?"

"That's right, someone else may have been involved and he thinks he may know who."

"It's Helga isn't it?"

"You knew?"

"Not for sure, but I have suspected she was involved in something."

"I think Frank may be ready to lay it all out for us when we get back."

"What's the plan for getting Gisela out of East Germany?" Frank asked before Jeff or Claude could say anything.

"Paul's been bugging me all day about it." Jeff explained the plan and how concerned he was about having someone that had never worked in the field involved.

"Don't be so worried about her," Frank said. "We all have to start somewhere. Six months ago I was just an innocent and naive agent also. If she is half as smart as you say she is she will be OK."

"I wish I had as much confidence in her as you do," Jeff said. "Now what is this new information you've dug up?"

"I have information that leads me to believe that someone else has been or is sending information to the East Germans. A lot of what they have been getting could not have been sent by Paul. He would have no way of knowing the information they have been getting. Most, if not all of it could have come only from Hodge's office."

"So you think Helga is involved?"

"Yes I do."

"Do you have any way of proving it?"

"Not yet, but I do have a plan. Here's a dispatch I want to send through. I don't believe that Helga knows yet about Paul and if this turns up in East Germany we'll know how it got there."

"Very well. Send it through."

"There's more. In looking through the papers I noticed that a lot of the information was not about this hospital. There's an indication here that the Russians know every time there's going to be an alert, and a lot of information about the units over in Baumholder. Also, one of the GI's here was in a whore house over there the other night, and he swears it was Helga he was with."

"How's that possible?"

"What do you mean how?"

"Wouldn't Helga have recognized him?"

"Not necessarily. She couldn't possibly know every man here."

"But the reputation she has of being an ice berg. Is it possible that you could have been so wrong about her? I had a feeling all along that she was not what she seemed, but I never suspected anything like this."

Helga may have had a reputation of being frigid, but none of the men that had tried to date her knew of her after office life. Helga was a regular at The Gentlemen's Club in Baumholder. She had started selling her body there shortly after she was hired by the 98th Hospital. If, as they say, practice makes perfect, then Helga was a fast learner. She was one of the most popular girls there. What her men friends didn't realize was that she was giving them much more than just her body.

A few years after she was raped, Helga noticed that something was wrong and went to a doctor friend for an exam. The doctor discovered that Helga had syphilis. Apparently at least one of the men that raped her had VD. The doctor told her it was too late for a complete cure, but he might be able to treat it and keep it under control for a while. "It might be several more years before you began to have or show symptoms," he told her. "Obviously you will infect anyone you have sex with," He added. Helga had been looking for a way to take revenge ever since the rape, and now she had one.

At first she was reluctant and repulsed at the thoughts of becoming a prostitute. The thought brought back the memory of seeing the fear and shame on her mom's face as the men threw her down on the bed and ripped off her clothes. It took a while to get over that and the thought of how invaded and vulgar she had felt when those same me took her virginity. However, the thought of sweet revenge blinded her to all that and she started spending all her evenings and nights in Baumholder.

When she saw Jeff walk into Hodge's office that day she thought her revenge might become even sweeter. She thought Jeff was CID and he reminded her of the agent that had laughed at her and said she must have done something to lure the soldiers on. It was time for payback, and the handsome agent walking through her office was going to be her target. That first night in Jeff's room when she told him that she had enjoyed it also, it wasn't the act she had enjoyed, but the thought of the revenge she thought she was getting that she had enjoyed.

Not long after Helga began working at The Gentleman's Club the Stasi had taken an interest in her and tried to recruit her. She wanted no part of that and turned them down. However, after she had time to think it over she decided she might be able to work out a deal with them, but only on her terms. After that, a Stasi agent was one of her regular customers. She got paid for the information she gave him, and he got more than he bargained for from her.

"Where do we go from here?" Jeff asked.

"I think we first need to give some thought to what's going on with Paul and Gisela," Frank said.

"Jeff mentioned that this whole thing may have been just a distraction," Claude said.

"I think that's exactly what it was." Frank said. "But, a distraction from what?"

"You have to include what has been going on with Helga and me." Jeff said. "I think the whole affair with her was to keep me occupied and from noticing what else might be going on."

"What might be going on? That's the question we need to answer right now." Frank said.

"Is it all that stuff about Baumholder?" Jeff asked.

"No. I don't think so. We've already been all over that. It's got to be more than the identity of some army units."

"What are we missing here?" Claude asked.

"It's been a long day. Why don't we all get some rest and continue this tomorrow? I think we may need to bring Harold into the conversation," Jeff said.

"I agree," Frank said.

EIGHT

OPERATION FREEDOM FLIGHTS

"Message Center," Frank said as he answered the phone.

"How about coming down to my supply room," Claude said. "I've got something I think you might be interested in."

"Be there in a few minutes." When Frank got to the supply room, Claude and Marvin were staring at a foot locker like they had never seen one before.

"That must be one interesting foot locker," Frank said.

"It's not the foot locker," Claude said. "It's what's in it."

"Wow!" Frank said as he looked in the foot locker and saw all the money. "Where did that come from?" He asked.

"We don't know," Claude said. "It was in the supply truck that came in this morning. Marvin found it while he was unloading the other supplies. As near as we can determine there must be over a hundred thousand Marks in here."

"Are they Reich Marks?" Frank asked.

"No, they're not Hitler money. They're the real deal. Genuine Deutsche Marks. Why?"

"I thought maybe someone had stumbled onto some old German army money. Maybe a payroll that never made it to where it was supposed to go."

"I don't think so," Claude said. "This is something else altogether."

The OD foot locker with Cpl Lloyd McDavid stenciled across the top and front in white lettering had been in a truck with all the other supplies that came in to the 98th that morning from the army supply depot in

105

Kaiserslautern. "Any idea how it came to be on your truck?" Frank asked.

"None what so ever. I've got a call into them now to see if they know anything about it."

"May I suggest that you don't say anything about the money when they call you back."

"Wasn't planning too. Would this be something you would be interested in looking into Frank?"

"Is the Pope Catholic?"

"I thought so. That's why I called you down here. Looks like you'll be spending some more time away from being a counterspy."

"And this time I won't have to worry about Bradley. Do you think you and Jeff can take care of the spy business for a few days?"

"I think we can handle it. However, my gut is telling me that it will be much longer than a few days."

The first thing Frank did was find out who Corporal McDavid was. A Corporal McDavid with the 278th Armored Infantry had been killed during a training exercise six weeks earlier. All of his personal belongings had been sent to the next of kin, and his foot locker and wall locker placed in a quartermaster warehouse in Darmstadt. The foot locker was now missing along with one of the Germans that had worked in the warehouse. Frank told the Quartermaster Captain he was talking to that he had found the foot locker, but didn't mention the money. He told him that it had shown up at the 98th General Hospital in Neubrücke with some supplies from their depot in Kaiserslautern. "Any idea how the foot locker got from your warehouse in Darmstadt to a supply depot in Kaiserslautern," he asked the Captain. "We didn't even know it was missing until we got your call yesterday," the captain said.

"Corporal McDavid was killed in a training exercise six weeks ago," Frank told Claude. "He was an APC driver with the 278th Armored Infantry Battalion. His foot locker was sent to a warehouse. The quartermaster folks don't have a clue how or when the foot locker went missing, and one of the

Germans that worked there hasn't shown up for work in more than two weeks. They don't know if there is a connection and I didn't tell them about the money. What did you find out from the folks in Kaiserslautern?"

"Nothing. They didn't know the foot locker was in the truck."

"I'm going to Darmstadt and talk to the quartermaster captain in charge of the warehouse. Can I borrow your car for a few days?"

"Sure. If I need any transportation I can always get something from the motor pool. You be careful Hoss."

Frank found out the Germans name was Martin Smitch. He had worked at the warehouse longer than the captain had been there and had never missed a day of work until two weeks ago. No one knew anything about the foot locker. While Frank was gone Jeff came by to see Claude.

"Where's Frank?" he asked. "I went by the message center to see him, and they told me he had gotten a three day pass to do some sightseeing."

"Yeah, that's the company line. He's really doing a little investigating down in Darmstadt."

"What kind of investigating?" Claude didn't answer. He just turned to the chest sitting under the window behind his desk and opened it.

"Wow! What's that all about?" Jeff asked.

"That showed up in a truck with all our other supplies the other day. There's over a hundred thousand Marks in there, and we don't have a clue as to where, what, or who. Frank did find out the man the trunk once belonged to is dead, and that it was in a warehouse in Darmstadt. He's down there trying to get some answers."

"Why Frank?"

"You don't know a lot about Frank do you? He's the trained investigator on this team. That's what he did as a civilian before taking this active duty gig. I'm just the sidekick in this act. The only thing I know about being a CID cop is what I learned by observing what the other instructors were doing back there at Gordon. I was an escape and evasion instructor and know nothing about being an army private eye. I don't know why I'm here. However, Frank has a degree in criminal justice, and he solved a murder case while he was still in CID school. He also solved a drug and black market caper just before you got over here. He doesn't like being a counterspy and will take on anything even remotely resembling wrong doing just to get away from it."

"Yeah, I heard about that drug thing, but didn't know he was that well trained. I guess this stuff about your being green and inept is just a cover, huh?"

"I guess," Claude said. "However, I don't think Bradley or anyone else knew that Frank was as capable as he is. What did you want to see him about?"

"I had some questions about that information he had about Helga's involvement in giving information to the East Germans."

"Anything I can help you with?"

"I don't think so. What I wanted to know was if he knew how Helga was communicating with them."

"I wouldn't know anything about that," Claude said. And, while they were talking Frank walked into the office.

"What'd you find out?" Claude asked before he could even find a chair and sit down.

"More than I wanted to," Frank said. "And, even more of a mystery. I'm glad you are here Jeff, you may be able to clear something up for me."

"I'll help any way I can," Jeff said.

"The missing Germans name is Martin Smitch. He is a war veteran and flew fighters for the Luftwaffe. He may be one of the last men alive that flew those German jets. He was a ME 262 pilot at the end of the war, and is credited with shooting down two B17's, a P47 and P51 with one of them. Before that he was a ME 109 squadron commander and an ace several times over. He was shot down twice and spent almost a month in the hospital getting over the last one. After the war, he tried to enlist in the US Air Corps, but they wouldn't let him in because of his German war connection. He loves to fly and has been taking on odd pilot jobs ever since the end of the war. He said if the price is right he will fly anything, anywhere, anytime. He is not connected in any way to that box full of money and knows nothing about how the foot locker may have left the warehouse. The reason he left was to keep from being killed. He was warned that some men were looking for him. He knows that a couple of his pilot friends have mysteriously vanished, and he thinks the Stasi may be looking for him because of a flying job he had with something called Freedom Flights. Ever hear of that Jeff?"

"Whoa!" Jeff said. "You are beginning to meddle now." Jeff had forgotten all about the questions he had for Frank.

"Don't give me any of that hush-hush shit. Martin told me some of it, and it sounds unbelievable."

"Not a word of this leaves this office or is ever mentioned again. I'm surprised Martin told you about it."

"He wouldn't have, but when I pushed him he mentioned it when explaining that the Stasi might be after him for making those flights."

"Freedom Flights was a program designed to help some scientific and other folks important to our side escape from East Germany," Jeff explained. "We, the agency that is, had four bases set up on our side of the line. Two in the US Zone and two in the British Zone. Flights would be made from those sites to out of the way places just inside East Germany. These were mainly old Luftwaffe air strips, and none of the trips were more than a hundred kilometers into East Germany. Most of the trips were made with B26 Bombers that had been converted to accommodate passengers. We used those because they were fast, very maneuverable, and could land and take off on those short air strips that had been built for fighters. They had been stripped of all guns and could be flown safely at low levels. Sometimes at just above the tree tops. Believe me, the guys that flew those trips for us were real daredevils. Because of all the guns being removed they had no way of protecting themselves if they were attacked, and they knew there was little or no chance of rescue if they were shot down. I wouldn't have made the trips for ten times what they were being paid. The Russians and East Germans knew the flights were being made, but never knew where or when. Because of that we got away with it for as long as we did. Our agents in East Germany would make all the arrangements and have the assets, as they were called, at the designated sites when the planes would come in. The flights were all made at night, usually in the wee hours of the morning, and they were never on the ground for more than ten to fifteen minutes. They never shut the engines down and in most instances were already rolling out for takeoff before the doors were closed or the assets had a chance to sit down. The man I'm working with to bring Gisela out of East Germany was one of the agents that arranged some of the flights. When the Russians decided they couldn't stop the flights by conventional means they started destroying the air strips. As we had fewer and fewer places to land, the flights became few and far between."

"Are those flights still being made?" Claude asked.

"Officially, no," Jeff said.

"How about unofficially?" Frank asked.

"No comment."

"Martin worked for the CIA and is now running for his life because of it. Isn't there something you can do for him Jeff?"

"I can make some calls, but I already know what they will say. Since the so called program he claims to have worked for did not exist. He does not exist."

"Bull shit." Claude said. "After all he did for the US you can't just ignore him."

"Like I said, I'll make some calls. If it were up to me, I'd give him a medal and a permanent job with the agency. We could use a few good pilots like him. Langley may not admit it, but those guys were real heroes. I'll also talk to Harold about it. How do we get in touch with him if I can work something out?"

"I'll let you know when the time comes," Frank said. "I wouldn't want him to have an accident while you're doing the investigating."

"I don't think I like what you are insinuating."

"Like it or not. We all know what I'm talking about. Hell, I don't even trust your bosses to keep their word after they say they will keep him safe. I wouldn't be at all surprised to find out that it was some CIA spooks that took care of his friends and are the ones looking for him. It seems to be a dangerous world out there when you work for the CIA and they no longer have a use for you."

"Will my and Harold's word be good enough for you?" Jeff asked.

"Like I said, I'll let you know when the time comes. No disrespect intended," Frank said.

"Yes you do," Jeff said. "But, I don't blame you."

"What happens with this foot locker over here now?" Claude asked.

"I'll do what I should have done in the first place," Frank said. "I'll follow the money. I'm going to start by going to the supply depot in Kaiserslautern. Someone there must have seen the locker. This is beginning to smell like a drug deal gone bad. I think that chest full of money wound up someplace it shouldn't have been. We may never know for sure."

When Frank got to the supply depot a Major there wasn't going to let him look around or talk to any of his troops. He changed his mind after Frank showed him his badge and threatened to have him arrested for interfering with a federal investigation. It took several days, but Frank finally found the men that had placed their supplies on the truck that morning. The foot locker was already on the truck when they got to work that morning they said. "We thought it was part of the supplies that had already been loaded, and didn't question it," they said.

"Who would have had access to the truck before that?" Frank asked.

"Only the driver that brought it up from the motor pool."

"Would you happen to remember who that was?"

"You have to be kidding. Ask around at the motor pool. We send supplies out of here all over Germany, and there are about twelve or fifteen regular drivers. It could have been any one of them"

Frank decided he was getting nowhere fast, but decided to try the motor pool anyway. It would take a heap of luck to find the one driver from that morning, and even more arm twisting to get him to admit to it. What do I have to lose he mumbled to himself as he walked into the motor pool. It was even more complicated than he thought. None of the drivers had regular routes. They simply showed up for work and the dispatcher gave them their trip for the day. However, he did learn one thing from questioning the drivers. None of them had put a foot locker in a truck that morning, or any other morning. One of the drivers did remember seeing the box and wondered what it was. It was in the back of the truck when he checked it out. He hadn't bothered to look in the box or was even curious about it. They all admitted that for the past several months boxes like that one, and even an occasional duffle bag was in the trucks when they got to work. They didn't know how or when these items were placed in the trucks. It had to be either the dispatcher of the motor pool sergeant Frank decided.

He would start with the sergeant. He was a grizzled old Master Sergeant with more hash marks on his sleeve than Frank could count. "How in hell would I know about bags or boxes being in the trucks when they leave the motor pool?" he asked. "Most of the time they are already gone when I get here." After talking to him for a while Frank decided that he was clean and would probably skin them alive if someone in his motor pool was placing the items on the trucks. Frank decided to level with him and told him what was going on. The old sergeant looked at him like he was crazy, and then told him that his dispatcher had been acting a little funny lately and seemed to have more money that he should have for his rank. "If he is involved, I want first crack at him." The sergeant said. "Give me a few minutes with him first." Frank said.

In the end it took both of them, but the corporal admitted to knowing about the boxes and duffle bags. He said someone would put them on one of the trucks and then tell him where that particular truck was supposed to go. He didn't know who the man was or how or when he put the items on the truck. He was paid to see to it that the truck was sent to a particular destination. Yes, he had become suspicious about what was going on, but as long as the pay was good and all he had to do was send the truck to a certain base he wasn't going to ask any questions. Everybody had some kind of scheme going on, why shouldn't he make a little extra money too.

He admitted that he was in trouble now because one of the foot lockers that was supposed to go to Frankfurt hadn't been in the truck when it got there. He had checked, and the trucks had somehow been switched that morning. He didn't know where the foot locker was. The people that had been paying him to send out the items for them were threatening to kill him if he didn't find their foot locker. He pleaded with Frank to please give him back the foot locker if he had it.

"I won't give you back the foot locker, but I promise to keep you safe and to testify at your court martial if you will help us round up the folks that have been paying you," Frank told him.

"How do I do that?"

"The Provost Marshal will be getting in contact with you. In the mean time just continue to act as if nothing has happened. The Provost Marshal will provide your protection and tell you what to do next." Frank then went to the base Provost Marshal and filled him in on what had been going on. He told Frank that he knew about the drug operation, but hadn't been able to shut it down. This was the break he was looking for. He would take it from there. Frank didn't tell him about the foot locker full of money sitting in Claudes office.

"What happened? What did you find out?" Claude was asking before Frank could even get out of the car.

"I now know how and why that foot locker showed up in your supply truck," Frank said. "However, who was responsible or who the money belongs to may never be known. A dispatcher at the Kaiserslautern motor pool was getting paid to send trucks to a particular location. He claims not to know who was putting the extra baggage on the trucks and he is in trouble because that foot locker showed up here. It was supposed to have gone to Frankfurt. I turned everything I had over to the Provost Marshal down there, but I plum forgot to tell him about that foot locker in there. Why that particular foot locker was used is strictly a fluke. After my visit to the quartermaster warehouse in Darmstadt, the captain decided to do some checking and found that several items were missing. One of his clerks was selling them to the Germans. He normally painted over or stenciled over the names, but somehow had missed this one. If not for that I would never have had a clue about where to start looking."

"What happens to the money if you don't find someone to claim it?" Jeff asked.

"Based on what I've found out I doubt anyone will claim the money. I tried not to leave any clues about where it was, and I don't think a drug dealer is going to show up here claiming the money is his."

"I've been thinking about that also," Claude said. "I guess now we wait a reasonable amount of time and then find a good charity home for it. That shouldn't be too hard the way things are here in Germany right now."

"What is a reasonable time?"

"I guess since we are the owners of the money we get to decide that. In the mean time, I'll put a lock on the box and start locking my office."

"I would like to make a suggestion about what to do with it," Jeff said. "I know a small town about fifty kilometers north of Frankfurt that was completely destroyed by bombs during the war."

"From experience, Jeff?" Frank asked.

"It was the nineteenth of August, 1944 and my thirtieth mission," Jeff said. "We were supposed to bomb the railroad marshaling yard in Frankfurt but it was completely cloud covered. That little town north of Frankfurt was our secondary target. There was supposed to have been a munitions plant there. When I came back over here after the war I had a chance to visit that town. I couldn't find any sign there had been a munitions plant there, and the people I talked to said there never had been one there. Anyway, the town was destroyed, including a school and church. Most of the kids in school that day had been killed along with their teachers. It took me several years to get over that experience. The money won't bring back any of those kids, but it sure would make me feel a little better if I could give that money to the town."

"What do you think Frank? Does that sound like a worthy charity to you?"

"You bet it does. If no one claims the money Jeff, it's yours, and I would like to be with you when you give it to them."

"Does this mean you will be back working with Claude and me now?" Jeff asked.

"Did you miss me?"

"Not really, but we do have some unfinished business to take care of, and after all, looking for spies is what you are getting paid to do."

NINE

MISSION ACCOMPLISHED

Alfred was waiting for Irma when she cleared customs. He introduced himself and handed her a packet of papers. Irma had expected a much older man and was surprised to see that Alfred was not much older than she was. He was also much more attractive than she had imagined him being. Alfred told her the papers would identify her and get her into East Germany and she would take the train to Gardelegen. Her tickets were in the packet and he would be on the train also but would not be in the same car. Irma found that she was attracted to Alfred immediately. That scared her more than the thought of what she was about to become and do. Although she had lost her virginity at a sorority party one night while she was a freshman in college she had not been with a man since. The thought of Alfred in that way frightened her and she wondered why. Alfred's touch to her elbow made her jump and they both apologized at the same time. The touch brought her back to reality and Alfred guided her over to a bench so they could talk.

After explaining to her the procedures for going through the East German customs and finding the train, Alfred told her to just act natural and he would see her on the train. Irma felt a moment of panic as Alfred got up and left, but it passed quickly as she reminded herself this was what she had wanted ever since becoming a member of the CIA, and Alfred would be watching her back. She couldn't help but wonder what he had thought of her. Had he had the same feelings about her that she felt for him? This is ridiculous she thought we just met. After regaining her composure, Irma got up and followed Alfred through the customs gate.

Irma had no problem getting through customs and finding the train. She was a little surprised at the ease she had with the language. She felt another moment of panic when she looked around and didn't see Alfred on the train as it pulled out of the bahnhof. Then she remembered him telling her he would be in a different car. Alfred didn't know whether to tell Irma the German Stasi had taken an interest in her and had placed an agent on the train. He decided it wouldn't do any good and might upset her too much. He decided just to keep an eye on the man and if he approached Irma he would take appropriate action. Irma didn't know it, but Alfred had been instructed to take whatever action necessary to keep her out of harms way. After meeting her and seeing how attractive she was he intended to do just that.

There were no incidents on the two hour train ride through the German countryside. The train made three other stops before reaching Gardelegen and Alfred was relieved to see that the Stasi agent didn't get off the train. Maybe he had been mistaken about the agent or maybe he had already notified other agents in Gardelegen. After looking around and seeing there was no one watching them Alfred gently took Irma's elbow and guided her to his car.

"I took the liberty of booking you into a hotel," he told her.

"Thank you," she said.

"It's within walking distance to the gasthaus where you are to meet Gisela tonight. I will also be there, but neither of you are to notice me."

"How will I know Gisela?"

"Don't worry. She will know you. Just make yourself comfortable and order a beer."

"I don't like beer," she said. That took him by surprise. "I thought your father was a brew meister?"

"He is, but I never developed a taste for it."

"Just pretend you are drinking. However, I think you will find the German beer much better than Schlitz." That remark surprised her. Just how much more did he know about her life?

"There's the gasthaus," he said as they drove past, "and just down the street there is the hotel. I won't go in with you just in case anyone is watching."

"Is there really a danger for that?" she asked.

"Oh yes," he said. "Around here there's a hundred percent probably that somebody is watching somebody. I have no doubt that everyone is being watched."

"Will that be true tonight when I meet with Gisela?"

"Yes. Does that bother you?"

"I don't know yet how I feel about it."

"It's a strange society in East Germany these days. Dangerous too." As soon as he said it he wished he hadn't added that dangerous part, but she needed to get used to that just being a part of what she had gotten into. The sooner she became aware of how different the world she had just entered was from the one she left the easier his job would be.

"Good luck, and don't worry. You'll do fine. See you tonight," Alfred told her.

He got out of the car only long enough to help her with her bag, and then he drove off. Wonder if I will ever see him again was her first thought. How stupid she said to herself. I'll see him tonight. Why am I so jittery? It's just natural somewhere in her brain answered back. What have I gotten myself into? You asked for this, so pick up the bag and act like an old pro came the little voice in her mind again. The thought seemed to calm her and she walked into the hotel and told the desk clerk she had a reservation.

Later that evening when she got to the gasthaus she picked a table in the back where she could see everything and ordered a wienerschnitzel mit kartoffeln and a beer. The waitress came back in a minute with her beer and told her that it would take a few minutes for her food. Irma thanked her and took a sip of the beer. To her surprise it was refreshing and tasty. Nothing at all like the harsh bitter taste she remembered from the Schlitz. Alfred had been right. She was almost finished with her meal when Gisela came in. Gisela looked all around the gasthaus carefully observing each of the more than a dozen patrons, then came straight to Irma's table. She was about to say something when Irma stood up and said, "Gisela?"

"Yes."

"Please sit down. My name is Irma."

Before either of them could say anything else, Irma saw Alfred come in and take a table on the other side of the room from them. After ordering a beer he began to look around. The same young couple he had seen the first night he was in there was at the same table and doing the same thing he had witnessed before. Alfred chuckled to himself and continued to look around. He didn't see anyone that looked suspicious, then he noticed the waitress on the phone. He immediately got up and while casually walking by Irma and Gisela's table he whispered, "the waitress may be an informer. Be careful what you say when she's around." He then walked on by and pretended to be going to the bathroom trying to listen to what the waitress was saying as he went by.

"Do you want to leave East Germany?" Irma asked Gisela after Alfred walked by.

"Yes"

"Would there be any complications to your leaving?"

"I don't understand what you mean?"

"What about your family?"

"I don't have a family. My father died soon after the war from injuries he received during a bombing raid on the factory where he worked. My mother never did get over the loss and died of a broken heart a few years later."

"Paul was told they were alive and you all were being held captive."

"So many lies."

"How long will it take you to be ready?"

"I could leave tonight." That answer took Irma by surprise. She looked over at Alfred's table and mouthed we need to talk. He shook his head that he understood. What Irma didn't know was that he had already decided they were going to have to chance a meeting since the Stasi had probably been told she was there and talking to Gisela.

"It will probably take us a couple of days," Irma said. "Will that be a problem?"

"No."

"Good. Here is the plan. We will leave on the train for Berlin. Somewhere during the trip you and I will change places. I will give you a new set of papers and ID and you will enter Berlin as me. I don't know if Alfred will be with you of if another agent will meet you after you make the crossing. Either way I will catch another west bound train and cross the border at some remote spot in central Germany."

"How will I know when we are leaving?" Gisela asked.

"I have to meet with Alfred to work out the details. Let's meet back here tomorrow evening and you will be told then what the final plan is." Gisela reached across the table and taking both of Irma's hands in hers she gave them a squeeze and with a loving smile she said, "thank you all for doing this for us. I know what a risk you are taking."

Jeff called Harold and told him that they needed to talk. "Good idea," Harold said. "I have some things I need to talk over with you anyway."

"Claude and Frank will be with me," Jeff said.

"OK!" Harold said. "Meet me at the Spiessbratenhaus in Idar tomorrow evening about seven. It's just north of town on the river. See you there.

When the men arrived Harold told them he had already ordered for them. We're having my favorite German meal. "Spiessbraten mit kartoffelin and beer," he told them. After having a few bites Frank said, "No wonder this is your favorite, it's delicious."

"I learned to eat this while I was growing up here before the war," Harold said. "My family never served this pork dish, but some of my friends families did and I loved to eat at their house."

"I never knew you grew up in Germany," Claude said.

"Yes, my family owned a jewelry shop here in Idar before the war. We left in a hurry in the middle of the night when the Nazi's came to town one night looking for Jews. I came back over here with the 1st Infantry Division. Signed on with the OSS after the war. But, that's enough about me."

"After my visit with you a few weeks ago," Harold said to Jeff. "I had a background check done on Helga. You're not going to like what they found. Shortly after the end of the war a group of black soldiers raped Helga and her mother."

"She told me about that," Jeff interrupted, "And when she reported it to the CID they laughed at her and wouldn't do anything about it."

"Did you also tell you that one of those men apparently had VD and that she now had syphilis?"

"Oops," Frank said. "You were weak and she was willing and now you'll be taking penicillin."

"Go to hell," Jeff said.

"Have you been using your kit?" Harold asked.

"What kit?" Claude asked before Jeff could reply.

"It's our standard issue kit," Jeff said, "For use in these situations. A small box of pills with instructions to take a good bath after the act, paying particular attention to that part of the body. Then, take two pills before going to bed and two more the following morning. So far it's kept me clean."

"Did you receive a kit like that Frank?" Claude asked.

"No I didn't, but maybe the CIA is sometimes called on to perform above and beyond."

"Yeah, or maybe when they say they are working under cover, they really are working under the covers," Claude said.

"See what I have to put up with, Harold?" Jeff said.

"Can we get back to business here?" Harold said. "And, Jeff, you go get yourself checked out just to be safe."

"We've had the Gentleman's Club in Baumholder put off limits and issued a warning for all the men who may have come into contact with Helga to get checked out. However, that won't protect all the men she may have exposed before this. All those men will have gone back home unaware of what they will be passing on to their girlfriends and wives as a result of a few minutes of pleasure. Looks like Helga found a way to get her revenge Jeff."

"Looks like it," Jeff said. "But, if she was out to infect as many soldiers as possible why wouldn't she go out with the men at the hospital?"

"Good question. My theory is that she didn't want to take a chance on someone finding out what she was doing. When you came along she thought you were CID and she could use you to really get back at them."

"My guess, for what it's worth," Frank said, "Would be that she didn't want to give away for free here what she was selling over in Baumholder. And, making a bunch of combat soldiers sick would do a lot more harm than doing the same thing to a bunch of clerks."

"Good point," Harold said.

"What happens now?" Claude asked.

"We have Stovall pick her up. We need to also find out about the information she may have been passing on to the Stasi."

"Why Stovall? Jeff asked.

"I don't want you getting involved."

"You mean blowing my cover?"

"Something like that."

"Did your background check uncover anything else about her?" Frank asked.

"No, why?" Harold asked.

"We think something else is going on besides her spreading a disease." Claude said.

"We think all those rumors and reports the East Germans have been getting may have been just a diversion to keep us from looking for something else." Jeff said.

"Even what Helga was doing?"

"Even that."

"Sounds interesting," Harold said. "Tell me what you have."

"When Bobby Joe made contact with Sergeant Lyons wife he found an entirely different situation than what we had been led to believe. She wasn't being held captive at all, and she had been told that Lyons was dead. It looks like the whole thing was made up to keep us looking in the wrong direction. I thought maybe that was what Helga was doing also. Keeping me entertained so that I wouldn't notice what was really going on."

"What is really going on?" Harold asked.

"That's the problem. We don't know."

"Do you have any theories or ideas?"

"None," Claude said. "We've gone over every possible angle and nothing comes to mind. That's a general hospital in the middle of nowhere and the most exciting thing that ever happens around there is trying to figure out what Hodge is going to come up with next. We've drawn a blank."

"Let me see if I understand what you are telling me?" Harold said. "Your assignments here were to find a spy or spies that were sending reports about the 98th Hospital to the East Germans. You have identified those responsible for that and they have been put out of commission. As far as I'm concerned you've accomplished what you were assigned to do. What's the problem?"

"Two problems," Jeff said. "One is we haven't gotten Gisela and our agents safely out of East Germany yet. Two, we've just uncovered a symptom; the real problem is still out there. All we found was the who. We still have to find the why. Like you told me some time ago, we still have a job to do."

"What's the status of that job in East Germany?"

"They should be on their way out. But until I hear they are all safe I won't be satisfied," Jeff said. "I was the one that gave the final go ahead to send that green agent in and until she is home safe and sound my job isn't over."

"You did what you had to do," Frank said.

"I know, and I didn't like it then and I still don't."

"Now you know a little of how I feel every time I have to send someone over there," Harold said. "Let's go to work on your other concern. Maybe it will help to take your mind off of Irma and Gisela."

"I've been hearing a lot of rumors about that Tactical Air Base in Birkenfeld," Harold said.

"What do you know about that place?"

"Not much," Jeff said. "My driver told me there was a small air force detachment there, and that he thought it was a communications center."

"We've been hearing those rumors also," Frank said. "I met a master sergeant the other night at a gasthaus over there who said he was stationed at the air base. Maybe I could run into him again and strike up a friendship."

"Sounds like a good place to start," Harold said. "Keep me informed. Also, Jeff those folks in East Germany are going to be OK. You've got to believe that. Believe me, it's the only way you can remain sane. We've all had a long day and I believe a productive evening. Let's call it a night."

"I wish I could be a confident about their safety as Harold is," Jeff said as they were driving back to Neubrücke.

"Like the man said, you have to believe that," Claude said. "Who was this sergeant you met Frank?"

"Tom Rogers. I got the feeling he was far more important to their project than he let on."

"What rumors?" Jeff asked.

"Your driver is right," Frank said. "That is a communications center. It is also an air control center. In fact, they provide air control for all allied air space over West Germany. About a year ago construction was started on what was advertised as an upgrade. Ever since then the rumor has been that what they are really doing is installing a top secret communications capability. So far no one has either confirmed or denied the rumors."

"What do you think?" Jeff asked.

"I think we need a lot more information about what is really going on."

TEN

JOE COLLINS

A week later as Jeff was sitting down for dinner in the hospital mess hall Frank and Claude got up from where they were sitting and came over to join him.

"Good evening gentlemen, please join me," He said.

"How well do you know Joe?" Frank asked.

"He was assigned to me when I got here. I don't know anything about him, why?"

"The body of Joe Collins was found in the woods behind the BOQ yesterday morning. The real Joe Collins," Frank said.

"A couple of nurses decided to go for an early morning walk and found the body. Major Stovall thinks it had been there for some time."

"My God!" Jeff said. "Who's been driving me around all this time?"

"We don't know," Claude said. "But, the real question is how did they know about your being assigned here?"

"How do you know the body they found is the real Joe Collins," Jeff asked.

"One of the hospitals ER doctors thought he recognized him when they brought him in and had the dental records checked. That ER doctor and Joe had become friends. They were regulars in some of the gasthauses around the area."

"This puts a whole new perspective on things doesn't it, Jeff said. "There's a lot more going on here than some innocent information about how many patients are in the hospital or what we are having for lunch. What are they after? Is it something to do with Baumholder?"

"We don't think so," Frank said. "We've checked that place out forty

127

ways from Sunday and there's nothing we can see they would be after there."

"What about those war games that are scheduled for next month?"

"We thought about that but can't see anything there either. The whole world knows about those games. It will be the first time since the war that both the German and French armies will be involved at the same time. It should be interesting, but hardly something to be spying on. The only new weapons that will be used is that Honest John Rocket and the Russians already know all about that and are building their own version of it. We don't think Baumholder is the target."

"The question right now," Jeff said, "is what are we going to do about all this? I think I better have a talk with Harold. I hate to bother him again this soon, but I think it's better he finds all this out from me. Besides, he needs to know there may be a leak somewhere and that's how they, whoever they are, found out about me and switched my drivers."

"I better drive you over there," Claude said.

"Good idea," Jeff said.

"Come in," Harold told them. "Saves me the trouble of trying to find you."

"Are you looking for me?" Jeff asked.

"I was about to start looking for you both. What's so important to get you out of the gasthauses and over here visiting a spook Claude?"

"We have something we think you should know about, and we need your help."

"Go on," Harold said.

"Joe Collins is dead, the real Joe Collins. His body was found in the woods behind the BOQ. Major Stovall said it had been there for a while."

"How do you know it's Joe?"

"One of the ER doctors he had been running around with recognized him when they brought the body in. They made a positive ID from dental records."

"That ties in with why I needed to find you," Harold said. "I just got this in from Washington." And he handed Jeff the dispatch he had received. Jeff read it and then handed it to Claude. The dispatch said that the DC police had pulled two bodies out of the Potomac a couple of weeks ago. The FBI thinks they were KGB and they may have been killed to keep them from talking. The two men had been on an FBI surveillance list. They suspect that the Kremlin found out the FBI was about to move in and took the men out before the FBI could question them."

"My God the KGB!" Jeff said. "What's going on?"

"We don't know," Harold said. "We don't even know if it's connected in any way with what's been going on over here, but the agency knew there was a mole somewhere in the organization. Maybe even working as a double agent. They don't know if those two were in any way connected to any of our projects. As for your driver, someone may have been tipped about your coming over here and they had your driver replaced. We just don't know all the facts right now, but until we do all our projects are on hold."

"What do we do about Joe or whatever his name is?" Jeff asked.

"See that he disappears as soon as possible. We don't know if he's connected with what happened in DC or if he is if he has been told about it. But if he is connected it will only be a matter of time until he does find out. I don't want him getting away. I want the bastard killed. But first I want you to find out what he knows and who hired him." Before Harold could say anything else Claude spoke up.

"Don't worry Jess, Frank and I will take care of it. Have him bring you by the supply room in the morning."

"I think we've done enough work for one evening," Harold said. "You all go on back to Neubrücke. Take care of Joe, or whatever his name is, and lay low until you hear from me."

"What's going on," Jeff asked as they were driving back to Neubrücke.

"That sort of muddies up the water doesn't it," Claude said.

"Man, it sure does. All along I thought it was the East Germen Stasi that was behind all this. Why would the KGB be involved?"

"I don't know, but I'm sure glad we didn't have Joe, or whatever his name is involved while we were tracking down what Lyons was doing."

"I hadn't thought about that," Jeff said. "Do you think my driver is a KGB man?"

"Doesn't matter if he is or not. You just bring him by my supply room in the morning. Frank and I will get some answers."

"I don't even want to know how," Jeff said as they were parking outside the BOQ.

"Good night Jeff,' Claude said and drove down the hill to his barracks.

While Jeff and Claude were gone Frank had decided to do some investigating on his own. Something about Joe's death was bothering him. He went to see Major Mirkleson in the hospital ER.

"Hi Major. Glad you're the one on duty tonight. If you have some time I would like to ask you a few questions?"

"About what?"

"About Joe?"

"What about Joe? And why are you asking?"

"Let's just say I'm the curious kind and let it go at that."

"No I won't. I've already told Major Stovall all I know about Joe."

"It's important Major. I can do this another way, but I don't want to have to do that."

"What's this about?"

"There's been an imposter posing as Joe and driving that state department man around."

"My God. Who are you?"

"I'm working for a government agency that's investigating Joe's death, and that's all I can tell you. When was the last time you saw Joe alive?"

"About a week, maybe ten days before they brought his body in."

"What did he tell you that last time you saw him?"

"He had been assigned to drive a state department special investigator around for a few days."

"Where did your last meeting with him take place?"

"In the O Club. Why are you asking me all this?"

"I'm trying to find out when and maybe where Joe was killed."

"We talked on for a while after he told me he would be driving a state department VIP around and then he left. I never saw him again until they brought his body into the ER."

"Who was Joe?" Frank asked.

"A friend," the major said.

"How did you know him?"

"We met one night in a gasthaus just after I got over here. I had gone out with a couple of the other doctors, and Joe was sitting at a table by himself when we went in. We sat down at a table next to him. I don't remember just how it happened, but one of the other doctors asked him if he spoke English and asked if he could settle an argument for us. He joined us, answered the questions, and before the night was over it seemed as if he had been one of us all along. A few nights later I saw him again and we became friends. Is that what you had in mind?"

"Well, yes and no. What I really wanted to know I guess is who was he?"

"I don't know that much about him. Although one night he had a little too much to drink and wanted to talk."

"He had been conscripted into the German army during the last days of the war. He was only sixteen years old then. After the war ended he went back home and found that his family, a father, mother and younger brother had been killed in a bombing raid. He blamed the Nazis for their deaths and didn't understand why he was not killed with them. He enrolled at the University of Heidelberg with some sort of a lend-lease grant and studied to become an English teacher. He was well on his way to becoming a principal. However, he became involved with the wrong woman and lost all he had worked for. She was the wife of the director of schools in Birkenfeld. She hadn't bothered to tell him she was married. Since then he has been unable to find a teaching position and managed to eat and pay for a small room by taking odd jobs, primarily for the American military."

"Joe Collins doesn't sound very German," Frank said.

"I asked him about that one night. His real name was Helmut Göering. They were distant relatives to the head of the German Luftwaffa. After he lost his teaching position and tried unsuccessfully to find work for the American military, he thought it might be the name. Joe Collins was a character in one of the English books he used in his classes. Helmut borrowed his name and got the next job he applied for. He had been Joe Collins ever since."

"Is that what you wanted to know?" asked the Major.

"Yes. That tells me that his death was not related to anything in his past. He was killed just so someone else could take that driver job. Why is another question?"

"What's going on here?" the major asked.

"I can't talk about that," Frank said.

"The hell you can't. I give you all this information and you can't at least give me a hint?"

"It's a matter of military security. Someone here at the hospital is giving information to the German Secret Police. You have to promise me you won't breathe a word of our conversation to anyone."

"I couldn't even if I wanted to," the major said. "I don't understand any of what went on here tonight."

"Good. Let's keep it that way."

"Wait a minute. That's it?"

"I think Joe may have been killed shortly after he walked out of the O Club that night. We don't know if the man that's been posing as him did it or not, but we will find out, and rest assured, whoever killer your friend will pay for it."

"I would appreciate it if you keep me informed, especially when you catch Joe's killer."

"Will do Major, and thanks again."

Uri Stefaslaf had been waiting outside the O Club for over an hour when Joe Collins came out. Two or three times he had almost been seen by some nurses walking up the hill from the hospital. Now as Joe came out and walked over to the car, Uri crouched down on the other side. He looked around to make sure no one was watching and when Joe started to open the door Uri made his move. Placing one hand around Joe's head and over the mouth to keep him from screaming out and the other on the opposite shoulder. One quick twist and he heard the bones in Joe's neck snap. He quickly loaded the body in the car and drove up the hill to the end of the road.

Uri had been over this area several times in the last few days and knew just where to park so the car would not be visible to anyone coming out of the O Club or the BOQ. This hill in the edge of the woods was one of several places he had checked out after being given the assignment. He quickly drug Joe's body into the woods and covered it with some brush. But, not before removing Joe's billfold and papers. A few minutes later Uri walked out of the woods and got in the car and drove back down the hill. The next morning at 0900 the new Joe Collins picked up Jeff McReynolds in front of the BOQ.

Uri had grown up in Washington DC during the 1930's He was the son of a soviet diplomat and they had been sent back to Moscow at the end of the war. Uri, now seventeen years old and speaking Russian with an accent didn't fit in with the Moscow youth that had endured the privations and misery that WW II had visited on the Russian people. He was looked on as an outsider. As a result, he started drinking and was soon in trouble. Instead of sending him to a gulag in Siberia a KGB agent had spotted something useful in Uri and offered to spare him a life in prison for his service as an agent. Uri had readily agreed and after a short training period had been sent to Germany. He had spent the last several months drifting around Germany, mostly in the gasthauses listening to the GI's.

When the Russians found out that another agent was being sent to the Birkenfeld region Uri had been assigned to keep an eye on him and find out why he had been sent there. Killing Joe and becoming Jeff's driver had been Uri's idea. Although killing was not unheard of in KGB operations, Uri had crossed the line. Even the KGB didn't kill just for the sake of killing. When they heard the body of the driver assigned to the state department agent Uri had been sent to watch had been found they knew

Uri was involved. It wouldn't take the Americans long to figure out what had happened and arrest Uri. It would only be a matter of time after that they would know of the KGB's involvement in this part of Germany. They couldn't let that happen.

When Jeff came out of the BOQ the next morning his car was parked by the curb, but he didn't see his driver. When he looked in the car the body of the man who had been calling himself Joe Collins was lying in the back seat. At first Jeff thought he had probably spent the night there, but when he tried to wake him up he realized he was dead. This is getting very intriguing he said to himself. He went back in the O Club and called Claude. It was only a matter of minutes before Frank and Claude along with Major Stovall arrived.

"Looks like someone did us a favor," Frank said.

"Maybe," Jeff said. "But, this sure complicates things doesn't it?"

"There is no noticeable cause of death," Stovall said. "We'll get him down to the ER and let those doctors have a look at him."

"I'll go with him," Frank said.

"This is probably the man that killed Joe Collins," Frank told Major Mirkleson as they brought the body into the ER. "Looks like someone didn't want him talking to us."

"Just as well," Mirkleson said. "I may have killed him myself if I got the chance."

"We need to know all you can tell us about how he died and when," Major Stovall said. Jeff, Frank and Claude were already heading for Claude's office when Stovall came out of the ER. I need to somehow get involved in that conversation he said to himself and started down the hill after them.

"What's going on here?" Stovall asked as he came uninvited through the door into Claude's office.

"What do you mean?" Jeff asked.

"Come on," Stovall said. "You admitted to Bradley that you were CIA.

The man that was assigned as your driver was murdered, and now the man who supposedly killed him is dead. What kind of fool do you take me for?"

"Don't get your fruit of the looms in a wad Major. I suppose you are entitled to some sort of explanation. The short version is we don't know what's going on with Joe and who ever that other fellow is, and with him now dead we may never know."

"I may be able to help out a little there," Frank said.

"How are these two involved?" Stovall interrupted and gestured towards Frank and Claude.

"They are CID," Jeff said.

"My God!" Stovall said. "There really is CID running around in Hodge's hospital, and I told him it was all just rumors. I knew all along you two were not what you seemed to be, but I never suspected CID. Just one question, why did you start those rumors?"

"We thought it might be fun to gore the ox a little," Claude said.

"You sure did that. I've never seen Hodge so wound up. I wouldn't want to be in your shoes if he ever found out"

"Can we get back to talking about what's going on around here?" Jeff asked.

"Sorry," Stovall said. "Go on with your story Frank."

"Joe Collins and Major Mirkleson were friends, and they were together at the O Club the night Joe was killed. Joe had told him that he had a job driving for some state department VIP that was going to be in the area for a few days. Joe had lost his teaching job in Birkenfeld and had been taking odd jobs for the army. It was just a coincidence that he was the one assigned to drive Jeff around. His death was a result of having that job. Whoever that fellow that's laying on a slab in the ER is, he was probably assigned to keep an eye on Jeff. Who gave him the job and why he is now dead is the mystery."

"We don't know if any of this had anything to do with what Sergeant Lyons was involved in or not," Jeff added. "But, what we do think is that all this may have been just a smoke screen to keep us from seeing what is really going on."

"What do you think is going on?" Stovall asked.

"Right now we don't have a clue," Claude said.

"Wait a minute?" Jeff said. "I just thought of something. Something has been bothering me about that man ever since that first day when he drove me around and I just realized what it is. When I told him I wouldn't be needing him for a few days and asked him how I could get in touch with him he told me to tell the bar tender at the O Club. How would the bar tender know how to get in touch with him and why would the CIA be using him?"

"Is that bar tender an agent?" Claude asked.

"He may be an agent, but he is not CIA."

"Are you sure?"

"Positive. Harold gave me a list of all the agents in the area and he is not on that list."

"It gets more interesting all the time doesn't it," Frank said.

"Any way to check him out Major?" Jeff asked.

"I'll see what I can do," Stovall said. "Any idea how he, or they found out about you coming over here?"

"A couple of KGB agent's bodies were pulled out of the Potomac a couple of weeks ago. They had managed to infiltrate our transportation office in DC, but the FBI had discovered what they were up to and put a watch on them. Someone must have found out and had them killed to keep them from talking. They could have alerted folks over here about me before they were killed."

"Could that be what happened to your driver?"

"What do you mean?"

"Could he have been working for the KGB and they had him killed to keep him from talking after Joe's body was found?"

"Could be," Jeff said, "but, all of this is just speculation."

"Do you have anything better right now?"

"Unfortunately, no."

"What did you mean up there at the O Club when you said it looks like someone did us a favor?" Stovall asked.

"We were going to get rid of him," Frank said.

"How?" Stovall asked.

"Fortunately, we won't have that to figure out now," Frank said.

"Now I remember you two. You made the front page of Stars and Stripes a couple of years ago," Stovall said.

"I didn't know you were trying to remember us?" Frank said.

"I've been sitting here trying to remember where I'd seen your names ever since Jeff told me you were CID."

"What was that Stars and Stripes thing all about?" Jeff asked.

"It's a rather long story," Claude said.

"We aren't going anywhere," Jeff said.

"It all started when a couple of the "good ol' boys" from the sheriff's office in Augusta, Georgia tried to railroad a GI at Fort Gordon," Claude said. "A body was found in the azalea bushes behind the fourteenth green about a week before The Masters Golf Tournament. The sheriff somehow decided that an MP at Fort Gordon was responsible. At his arraignment the Provost Marshal worked a deal with the judge to have him released to his custody. That really pissed the sheriff off and the feud between the county "good ol' boys" and the military police was on."

"That's it. You made the front page of Stars and Stripes with that?" Jeff said.

"That's the short version," Frank said.

"I don't care about any short version," Jeff said. "I want the whole story."

"Sergeant Ed Ramey was an MP at Fort Gordon. He liked his beer and he liked to party," Claude said.

"Sound like anyone you know Jeff?" Stovall interrupted him.

"Could be," Jeff said.

Claude didn't miss a beat. He just laughed and continued. "Frank's class was in their last week of advanced training and I was one of their instructors. Because of his partying, Ed had been in trouble with the sheriff's office on several occasions before. In fact, the Provost Marshal had to bail him out of jail more than once for his escapades. A couple of the grounds keepers were getting the course in shape for the Masters and found the body of a young girl hidden in the bushes behind where the grandstand was being assembled behind the fourteenth green. During their investigation the sheriff's office found out that Ed and the young lady had been sharing a beer in one of the local watering holes and had left together. That's the last time anyone had seen the girl alive. The school commandant decided that since it involved a GI, investigating the case would make a good class exercise. He assigned me to oversee the operation and grade the students. After reviewing the evidence, all of the students but one came to the conclusion that Ed was guilty."

"Let me guess?" Jeff said. "Frank was the lone holdout."

"A couple of deputies came to the base and arrested Ed," Claude continued. "When the Provost Marshal heard about it he went to the judge and convinced him that due to Ed's previous history with the sheriff's office it wouldn't be safe for him in jail. The judge agreed and released Ed to his custody. Ed was confined to the base until the trial. The sheriff was so hot you could have lit a roman candle on his face when that happened. After Frank wanted to continue the investigation the school commandant, who was a member at the Augusta National Golf Club got permission for Frank to visit the site where the body was found. Someone alerted the sheriff, but not before Frank and I had a chance to have a good look around. By the time the sheriff got there we had looked all we needed to. The sheriff had us escorted off the golf course and had the judge to declare it off limits to us. Ed never denied being with Linda that night. He told Frank that he had met her at the road house and after a few beers had taken her home, but he said she was very much alive when he left her apartment sometime around three in the morning. Ed also told Frank something else. Linda and one of the deputies had been dating some and had only recently broken up. The bar tender at the roadhouse told Frank it wasn't a pretty site when that happened. The sheriff had forgotten to mention that to us when we were talking to him. While we were nosing around at the golf course before the sheriff ran us off I noticed Frank picking up something. Just an ordinary button I told him. But, it's almost new he said, not weathered at all. After we got back to the base the Provost Marshal agreed to send the button off to the crime lab in DC. It turned out to be a very special button. Only found on the uniforms of police departments, sheriff's officers and class A military uniforms. Frank went back to the road house and asked if Ed was ever in his uniform while visiting there. Never, the bar tender told him. Frank then cooked up a plan and we went to the sheriff with it. After telling the sheriff about his deputy and Linda, Frank also told him about finding that button. We're going to be getting a court order to examine all of your uniforms he told the sheriff. For the next couple of weeks our class assignment was to keep watch on some of the deputies and go through their trash when they set it out for pickup. One of the soldiers came in a few days later holding up a deputy shirt with two missing buttons. The Provost Marshal confronted the sheriff with the shirt and told him he had already requested the Georgia Bureau of Investigation to investigate his office. He then presented the Judge with the evidence and the judge threw out the case against Ed. Stars and Stripes picked up the story and Frank and I had our few minutes of fame."

"I have an idea you left out some of the more juicier details," Jeff said. "But, it was still a compelling story. You're not as green and inept as you like to have everyone believe are you?"

"Please don't spread that around," Claude said. "It would ruin our reputation."

"How is the Lyons operation coming along?" Stovall asked as soon as Claude finished his story.

"We've located Gisela, and she and our agents will hopefully be out of East Germany in a few days," Jeff said. "Also, we have taken George into custody. We picked him up delivering a message for Lyons at the commissary. We had a couple of women stationed there to watch and they let us know when he came in. A bag boy was his contact there. He is innocent of any wrongdoing. He had no idea of what was going on, or what he was doing.

His only job was delivering the notes. George was paying him more than he made in a month for each delivery. As for George, we think he was acting entirely alone, but we haven't been able to find out who he was working for yet. There was a small radio receiver and transmitter in his room and that's how he delivered the messages to someone over in East Germany."

"Do you think he will talk?" Stovall asked.

"Oh yes. I think he will be singing like a bird before too much longer."

"Do you still think Lyons was the only one involved in sending information?"

"You brought that up once before," Jeff said. "What do you have in mind?"

"Just feeling you out. I think you know more than you are telling me."

"Alright. We do think someone else was sending out reports, but she was not connected with what Lyons was doing in any way."

"She?"

"Oops. Yes, she. It's Helga."

"I thought so," Stovall said. "How much do you know about her involvement?"

"It's a little embarrassing."

"Come on Jeff. Everyone at this hospital knows about you two."

"That's not exactly what I meant," Jeff said. "It seems there is a lot more to Helga than meets the eye. She is not what she seems. She is a prostitute working at The Gentlemens Club in Baumholder, and she has syphilis."

"My God?" Stovall said. "Have you been infected?"

"Fortunately not, but we don't know how many others may have been. She did it on purpose to get even for some soldiers raping her and her mother."

"I didn't know," Stovall said.

"No one knew," Jeff said. "In addition to that, we have evidence that she was also passing on sensitive information from Hodge's office. Frank used some creative writing and sent a special packet through the message center to Hodge. Everything he had in the packet showed up a few days later in East Germany." Claude said.

"How do you know Hodge wasn't the one that sent it out?" Stovall asked.

"He wasn't in his office at the time," Frank said. "He had been gone for over a week. No way could he be the one. We also think she may have been passing on information she heard from GI's during her 'work' at The Gentlemen's Club.

"Do you know how she has been getting the information out?"

"No. We don't think it was by radio like George was doing with the stuff he got from Sergeant Lyons. Nothing Helga might have been sending over was ever picked up that way. We are pretty sure that George was sending his information to a KGB agent. Helga is dealing with the Stasi. We have a mole in one of the Stasi offices and that's how we found out about what she is doing."

"Another thing we don't know is if what she is doing was the reason for the smoke screen Lyons was involved in," Claude said. "We now know that operation was just a ruse, that's the reason the radio was used. They wanted us to hear it."

"So you don't know what all she might have passed on to them, or if there is another agent here that she is working with?" Stovall said.

"That's about it," Jeff said.

"Could it have been this fellow that been masquerading as your driver?"

"I don't think so, but we'll soon find out won't we?"

"How so?"

"If nothing shows up over there for a while we can assume that it was my driver."

"I have a better idea," Stovall said. "Why don't I tell Hodge about her and have him set up a different method of receiving his communications."

"No way," Jeff said. "If there is another mole here we want to catch him. Leave things as they are. I'll put a watch on her. She won't get anything else out without us knowing who and how."

ELEVEN

THE TRAIN RIDE

fter Gisela left the gasthaus that night Irma got up and walked over to Alfred's table.

"What's wrong he asked?" as she sat down.

"She wants to leave right now."

"What did you tell her?"

"I told her we would have to discuss it and decide what we were going to do."

"Did she tell you why she wanted to leave now?"

"What she said was that she could leave any time."

"Good. I think the sooner the better. I'll make the arrangements. Did you tell her what the plan was?"

"Yes."

"Do you know how to get in touch with her?"

"Yes. She gave me her address."

"First thing in the morning go and see her and help her get packed. We will plan to leave on the afternoon train. The tickets will be waiting for you."

Alfred paid for their drinks and then took Irma to her hotel. She was disappointed when he let her out without making a pass or asking about going up to her room with her. She was beginning to wonder if there was something wrong. His being all business made him even more attractive to her. He wanted to do more. She could see it in his eyes when he looked at her. What was wrong that he didn't? The next morning she checked out of the hotel and took a taxi to Gisela's apartment. "I guess this means that we are not meeting back at the gasthaus tonight," Gisela said as she was showing Irma into her apartment. Irma noticed that she had already started getting ready. Irma told her to pack only what she needed and to use her bag since she was going to cross the border as Irma. Alfred had instructed Irma to take a taxi from Gisela's to the bahnhof and he would follow. As the taxi with the two women pulled out, the two men Alfred had been watching followed. That's what I was afraid of he said to himself.

Irma was a little uneasy when she didn't see Alfred at the bahnhof or see him get on the train. However after the train pulled out he walked through their car and motioned for Irma to follow him.

"I don't want to alarm you," he said to her as they were standing in the space between the two cars.

"Two men are following you. They are genuine Stasi agents. Very dangerous. One is in the car behind you and the other is in the car in front. They'll have to be dealt with since they can identify Gisela at the border crossing."

"What are you going to do?"

"I don't know yet, but I'll try to let you know before it happens. However, if I can't, or anything happens to me, don't try to take Gisela into West Berlin. I don't know what they might do, but we can't take that chance. Somehow disappear into the crowd at the bahnhof and then return to Gardelegen and wait for further instructions."

"I don't want anything to happen to you," she said, and then she would never know what made her do it, but she leaned over and kissed him on the lips. Alfred couldn't resist and took her in his arms and returned the kiss. He didn't want it to end and neither did Irma. Reluctantly he pushed her away and said, "You better go back and sit down while we still have our senses about us. I'm sitting just back of you next to the exit. I'll let you know what happens next."

Although at that moment he couldn't think of anything but holding Irma in his arms. How soft and yielding she had been and how those lips that he had been wanting to kiss ever since watching her walk off that plane several days before had felt. He would not let anything happen to either her or Gisela. Of that he was now sure. While he was sitting there thinking about what had just happened, the agent from the car behind them walked through their car. Just before exiting the car he turned and looked back. Watching him gave Alfred the idea he had been looking for. While thinking about it, he wondered what made the agent get up and go to the other car. Alfred wished he could hear what they were saying.

Since the agents were obviously watching them, it wouldn't matter if they saw Alfred and Irma talking. Alfred got up and asked Gisela to trade seats with him for a few minutes. As they were swapping seats the German agent came back into the car. He didn't understand what was going on and stood in the doorway and watched. He seemed relieved when they had all sat back down, and Alfred gave him a smile and wink as he passed by them on the way back to his car.

"I told you I would let you know as soon as I figured out what I was going to do," Alfred said. "When we get to the next stop I want both of you to get off. The next train will be coming through in less than an hour. Walk around the station, even the town, anything to kill some time. Then catch the next train to Berlin. They won't be expecting that, so you will be safe."

"But won't he see us get off or be waiting for us when we come in on the later train?" Irma asked.

"You're just full of questions aren't you?" Alfred said. "I'll stand in front of the door so he can't see you and if he does I'll block the door so he can't get out. If they do manage to warn Berlin and put them on alert, they'll be looking for two women, not a single woman party member on official business. Gisela will get through OK, and you will be just another woman looking for her husband in all the confusion. I'll go on in to Berlin and arrange a little surprise for them. Don't worry. If I thought for a minute you were in any danger I wouldn't let you get off the train. They'll probably be going crazy wondering what happened to you. I want you to wait until the last second before getting off the train. Then, when you get to the bahnhof in Berlin pay no attention to anything that may be going on around you. If my plan works the bahnhof will be crawling with agents, both theirs and ours. There's safety in confusion. Don't worry, I'll be there and looking after you. See that Gisela gets to the West Berlin crossing. One of our agents will be waiting for her on the west side. After seeing her go through, you go back to the gate where you just came in and pick up our tickets. They will be made out for Frau and Herr Alfred Lowden. I'll meet you just before the train is scheduled to leave. The tickets are for our trip to Brussels, Belgium where we will be going to the Worlds Fair. All the papers will have been arranged and be with the tickets. If anything and I mean anything goes wrong, abort immediately and get Gisela back on a train for Gargeleden. I'll try and get to you and help. Our mission is to get her out of East Germany, but not endanger her or ourselves any more than we have to in the process. Your and her safety right now is the most important thing to me."

"As soon as you can after getting off the train find a phone and call this number," Alfred said handing her a card with a phone number on it. "When they answer the phone, no matter who it is, say – the trains run on time. They will say back to you we've got the tickets. If you don't get that reply, hang up immediately and catch the next west bound train for Gargeleden. Have you got that? "

"I think so," Irma said.

"I know it doesn't make much sense, but it's a code letting them know that everything is going according to plan, and for them to send in the Calvary. If this works, those Stasi agents won't know what hit them. Now go and explain to Gisela what we are doing. Everything's going to be OK."

By the time Irma got back to her seat and had explained to Gisela what was going on the train was slowing down for its next stop. Irma and Gisela waited until the very last minute before starting for the door. Alfred followed them and then stood in front of the door window to the other car as the two women stepped off the train just as it started pulling away from the bahnhof. Just before stepping off the train Irma turned to Alfred said, "You be careful. I'm looking forward to my train ride to Brussels with you as Frau Lowden," and she brushed his lips with a quick kiss. The German Stasi agent never saw the women leave. Alfred went back to his seat praying there would be a phone close by and his plan would work.

The train hadn't much more than gotten back up to speed when the Stasi agent came back through the car. A look of panic crossed his face when he realized the women were gone. He practically ran to the other car, and both agents returned in a few minutes. After looking around they came to Alfred's seat and asked him to stand. "Where are the women?" One of them demanded.

"What women are you talking about?" Alfred answered.

"The two women you were with."

"I wasn't with any women."

"You got on the train with them in Gargeleden and you were talking with one of them."

"Two women did get on the train when I did, but they were not with me."

"What were you talking to her about?"

"It's none of your business, but I was asking her to go out with me when we got to Berlin. As to what happened to them, I don't know. While we were stopped back there I stepped out to have a smoke, and when I got back in here the train was moving and they were gone. I guess she didn't want to go out with me."

"You are lying," the agent that was obviously in charge said.

"You go to hell," Alfred told him and sat back down.

By now he was hoping they would try and do more than just talk. What they didn't realize was that he had his hand on his weapon the whole time they were talking to him, and he wouldn't have hesitated to use it. He had already put two of their agents in the Elbe River and throwing these two off the train wouldn't bother his conscious at all. In fact, he hoped they would try something. It would make the job in Berlin that much easier. The two agents must have sensed that he was ready and willing for a fight. "It's not worth it," one of them said and they left.

Bobby Joe Knight had grown up in the mountains of northeast Georgia. He graduated from high school the day the war in Europe ended. After spending a few days celebrating his coming of age he enlisted in the marines. Two months later he was on a troop ship bound for Guam. His unit, the 2nd Marines, was scheduled to be in the first wave of the invasion of Japan. Just before the ship reached port, Colonel Tibets and his crew in the Enola Gay dropped the A Bomb on Hiroshima, and the war was over. After spending eighteen months as part of General MacArthur's occupation forces in Japan, Bobby Joe returned to Georgia. The quiet life in the little village where he grew up no longer provide the excitement an ex-marine needed, so when the OSS recruiter came through town he signed up. Nine months later Bobby Joe Knight, north Georgia mountain accent and all, was in the Bavarian Alps in southern Germany looking for spies.

The area in the Bavarian Alps known as Obersalzberg was purchased by the Nazis in the 1920's as a playhouse for their senior leaders. Hitler and several of his top generals, Herman Göring, Martin Bormann, Heinrich Himmler, and Joseph Goebbels, his Propaganda Minister, built elaborate houses on a mountain there near Berchtesgaden. For Hitler's 50th birthday in 1939, the Nazis used slave labor to construct the Kehlsteinhaus on top of one of the mountain peaks. This party house, nicknamed The Eagle's Nest by a French diplomat, became Hitler's favorite getaway location. Berchtesgaden and its environs were fitted to serve as an outpost of the German Reichskanzlei (Imperial Chancellery) offices. An SS barracks was built on the mountain near the general's houses to provide protection for them when in residence there, and the area became a strategic objective for Allied forces.

The only way to reach The Eagles Nest was by a narrow one lane road up the mountain from where the SS Barracks was to the face of a sheer cliff about four hundred feet below the top of the mountain. From there a six hundred foot tunnel had been blasted through the solid granite rock, ending directly under the building on top of the mountain. There was an elevator for the final four hundred feet up to the building. The elevator shaft was also through solid rock. The allies never knew of its existence until its discovery by elements of the 101st Airborne Division during the last days of the war.

What no one in the little community near Berchtesgaden, not even Henrich's family, knew was that during the war Henrich had worked for the British MI6. Not real spying, just keeping his eyes and ears open and reporting what was going on in the area. He kept the little radio transmitter they had supplied him with hidden in his barn loft. His messages to them were short and infrequent. The Gestapo knew someone in the area was sending out coded messages, but could never pinpoint where the transmissions were coming from. Henrich's job was to let the allies know when Hitler and his generals were in the area. Sometimes his message would be only one word, yes, to let the folks listening back at MI6 know that the Nazis were in Berchtesgaden. Because of Henrich, American B17's and B24's had been scrambled several times for bombing missions to the area. All the houses and the barracks suffered extensive damage. However, none of the intended targets, Hitler or the generals, were ever killed or injured. After the war, Henrich destroyed the little radio and had gone about his business as if nothing had ever happened.

After the war the partially destroyed SS barracks was rebuilt and became the General Walker Hotel. It was used as an R&R location by the American occupation forces. That's why Bobby Joe was sent to the area. It was known that East German Stasi agents often frequented the hotel in hopes of picking up some idle gossip by the GI's on leave there. Bobby Joe had been sent there to sniff them out. The hotel might have been a good place to spend the night, but it was hardly the place to spend an exciting evening and Bobby Joe had started scouting out the gasthauses in the surrounding villages.

When he had told Irma about the dangers associated with the East German Stasi Agents, he knew from sad experience what he was talking about. He had only been in Bavaria for a few weeks when he met Herta. She had immediately captured his heart. Henrich's daughter, Herta, was a waitress in one of the gasthauses near Schönau am Köngsee on the German – Austrian border. After that first night when he saw her, he began spending all of his free time there. Herta had grown up in the little village and because of its isolated location she never knew any of the savagery of the war and very little of the shortages and hardships so many of the other Germans had endured. Being mountain folks they were used to living off the land and making do with what they had. The first American soldiers she saw was when some troopers from the 101st Airborne Division came through the area looking for German deserters after the war. That gasthaus was the last place Bobby Joe, or any other American agent for that matter, would have expected to find a Stasi agent.

When he saw the man walk into the gasthaus that evening Bobby Joe couldn't believe his eyes. Dressed in leather lederhosen, a plaid shirt, and long woolen socks and carrying a suitcase he looked like a character out of a novel. But, when he set the suitcase down on a table, opened it up and took an accordion out of it, wonder turned to amazement, and he soon had the place rocking. Playing for the few Marks, Pfennigs and occasionally a few dollar bills the patrons placed in the brass pot at his feet, he became a regular attraction at the gasthaus. As word spread about the accordion player the crowds grew, and soon on most nights it was standing room only.

Bobby Joe would never know what made him suspicious, but something about the accordion player was not right. The way he looked at people, some of the questions he asked during his breaks, something, maybe all of those things together told Bobby Joe to be suspicious. Anyway, he started watching what was going on more closely. No one around the gasthaus or even around the community had ever seen the man before, or knew where he came from. The more he observed, the more suspicious he became, and it all came to a head one night when he heard the accordion player asking

Herta about her family. Questions that even he had not asked her. Later that night while he was walking her home he asked her about the questions. He wanted to know why the man would be so interested in her family, and he told her to be careful because he didn't trust the man.

As Bobby Joe and Herta were walking up the lane to her house he sensed something was wrong. Just as he was about to say something the accordion player came out of the house. Herta was the first to speak, asking what was going on. The Stasi agent heard her and started shooting. Bobby Joe shoved her to the side and returned fire. His aim was deadly, and after only that first exchange of shots, the Stasi agent was dead. When he got back over to where Herta was laying he realized that she too had been killed. He was devastated when he realized he had probably killed her by shoving her into the accordion player's line of fire. After checking on Herta, he went to the house and found that the Stasi agent had accomplished his mission. Everyone was dead.

Bobby Joe's effectiveness as an agent died with Herta, and he was sent back to the states. Both he and the agency were surprised at how fluent in German he had become just by his conversations with Herta. He was sent to language school and taught how to get rid of his north Georgia accent. He remembered Herta laughing at the way his southern drawl made his German words sound. The first time he had tried to say ich liebe dich she had laughed so hard she cried. It hurt him to think she was laughing at him for saying I love you, but realized she was not laughing at him for loving her, but the funny way his accent made it sound. After nine months in language school, he was back in Germany. This time as Alfred Lowden, and in East Germany along the Iron Curtain Border to obtain information about the buildup of Russian troops. One night in a gasthaus a couple of Stasi agents had a little too much beer and threatened him. Afraid was afraid of having his identity exposed and left rather than confront them. However, he was waiting when they left the bar a few minutes after he had, and the two agents wound up in the Elbe River.

The two agents on the train that afternoon reminded him of that incident, and he was surprised at how much he was wishing they would try something. He was just itching to put a bullet in them and throw them off the train. Then he realized what his job was and how such an incident like that might blow the chance of Irma and Gisela's escape. The thought of that made him sit back down and shut up. He was relieved when the two agents walked off. He would deal with them later if he got the chance.

After they had gotten off the train, Gisela showed Irma where to find a phone. After Irma made the call Gisela said. "This is Potsdam. There is a good museum of the war here. It's just down the street from the bahnhof. We can spend our time there, and we'll be safe there."

"Good idea," Irma told her. They spent an uneventful forty five minutes looking at WW II artifacts, including pictures and documents from the conference that took place in Potsdam at the end of the war when the three allied powers decided the fate of post war Germany. The two women returned to the bahnhof just in time to catch the next train for Berlin.

Alfred spent an anxious forty five minutes wondering what the Stasi agents would try next. He was relieved when the train started slowing as it entered the outskirts of Berlin. Before getting off the train he gathered up as many papers as he could find and then gathered up several more from the benches inside the station. He scouted around, looking for the best place to create the diversion he had in mind, and saw the trio of other American agents scattered around. He gave them a thumbs up to let them know the plan was working and wanted to tell them what was about to happen, but didn't dare take that chance. He hoped they understood. Just before the train Irma and Gisela were on arrived, Alfred made his way into a rest room near the gate where the women would be coming in. He carefully wadded up the papers and stuffed them into a waste can and placed it in the middle of the room. He sprinkled some water on the papers so they would produce a lot of smoke and wouldn't burn so fast. He then set them on fire and on exiting the room he found the nearest fire alarm and broke the glass and pulled the ring. In spite of all his planning he wasn't prepared for the din he set in motion. He had never experienced sirens and the claxon horn sounding so loud or the stampede of people rushing to exit the building. He looked up just in time to see Irma and Gisela coming towards him fighting their way through the wave of people trying to make their way out of the building.

He thought he caught a glimpse of one of the agents trying to follow the two women before he was caught up in the mass of folks heading for the exit. He never saw him again. He motioned for the two women to move over near a wall, and when he reached them he told them to make their way along the wall to the customs gate. He then headed for the west bound trains ticket window.

Irma guided Gisela to the customs booth and saw the man standing just beyond in the American Zone. He smiled at Irma and gave her a thumbs up. Irma hugged Gisela and wished her luck and then stood and watched as she made her way through customs and to the agent that was waiting for her on the other side. Gisela turned and mouthed, thank you, then took the agents arm and left. After watching Gisela walk away, Irma headed for the gate where the train for Brussels would be leaving in only fifteen minutes.

The whole thing had take only minutes, but it had seemed like hours. Never had Alfred or Irma witnessed such a fire drill. By the time the firemen had the fire under control and the Stasi agents realized what was happening, Gisela was on her way to freedom and Frau and Herr Lowden were on their way to Brussels.

Somewhere between Gargeleden and Hanover as the train rumbled west through the German night Alfred switched off the lights and was crawling into his bunk when Irma told him to move over and crawled in naked beside him. He turned to face her and as she kissed him he moved his hand from her shoulder and caressed her right breast. As her tongue pushed past his lips and entered his mouth he felt her nipple begin to swell. He rolled her swollen nipple between his thumb and finger and moved his other hand down her body to the moist area between her legs. As soon as his fingers touched her there she reached for the hardness that was pressing against her thigh and guided him into her. It was going to be a pleasant trip through the East German night. Tomorrow would not only bring another day, but new dangers when they crossed the border into West Germany, but neither of them was concerned with that now.

The agent took Gisela to the Tempelhof Airport where she spent the night. She took the courier flight to Frankfurt the next day where Paul was waiting for her. He couldn't believe that after all these years and all he had been through these past few months they were finally together again. They moved into a room at The Four Daughters. Sergeant Lyons was as happy as he had ever been, but he also knew the story wasn't over yet. It wouldn't be until the army handed down its final decision about whether he was guilty of treason or not. Both Major Stovall and that Mr. McReynolds had promised him they would do all they could for him, but the final decision would be up to Colonel Hodge. Sergeant Lyons knew that could go either way and wasn't going to do any celebrating just yet.

When Winston Churchill said that an Iron Curtain had descended across Europe, he knew what he was talking about. Almost as soon as the partitioning lines had been drawn dividing post war Germany into four zones of occupation the Russians closed off their section to the rest of the world, including Berlin which was 100 miles inside the Russian zone. The Soviets had granted the allies only three air corridors for access to Berlin, and they had never formally agreed to rail or road access. However, they did allow the use of one rail line and some road and canal traffic. In June, 1948 the Soviets closed all rail, road and canal access to the allied sectors of Berlin. In response, the allies organized the Berlin Airlift. In what the allies called Operation Vittles, just nine months later the airlift was delivering more cargo into Berlin than had ever been brought to the city by rail. A month later the Soviets lifted the blockade but still maintained strict control over all traffic in and out of the Soviet zone. For example, when a truck convoy crossed the border it was timed to its destination. Any deviation from the normal time required for travel was met with strict punishment, sometimes resulting in imprisonment.

The Berlin airlift might be over, but not the strict control over all traffic in and out of East Germany from the allied sectors. The Soviets might have lost face over the Berlin Airlift, but East Germany remained closed to the rest of the world. All passenger rail traffic going west from Berlin was stopped at the border. All passengers going any farther had to leave the train, and go through a customs station to get on another train on the western side of the border. Only those folks with the proper papers were allowed to proceed. While Alfred and Irma were walking towards the customs booth after their overnight train ride Irma asked Alfred, "If he was going to start another fire?" After a polite laugh he told her, "That won't be necessary this time. They won't be looking for Frau and Herr Lowden. As far as they will be concerned we are just another couple on our way to the Worlds Fair in Brussels, and we have our tickets and papers to prove it. I doubt they have even been alerted to what happened in Berlin last evening."

Once they were safely out of East Germany, Alfred found a phone and called Jeff. At about the same time the courier flight bringing Gisela from Berlin was landing in Frankfurt the next morning, Jeff received word that Alfred and Irma had crossed the border safely into the British Zone. Irma had earned her wings. She was sent back to Langley where she went through the complete six months training cycle to become a CIA field agent.

Everyone thought that Colonel Hodge was a bumbling old relic left over from the war. He was that, but what they didn't know about him was what had caused him to be so bitter and calloused. Major Hodge had been the battalion commander of one of Patton's tank battalions when they broke through the German lines and relieved the 101st Airborne Division at Bastogne. A proud Major Hodge had expected to receive an award for his leadership and actions there. Instead, he had received a reprimand and was relieved of his command. He barely escaped a court martial for dereliction of duty. He had misinterpreted an order and instead of attacking when the regiment was ordered too, he held his battalion in reserve. In spite of his heroic efforts to drive back a German Panzer attack just two days earlier that his regimental commander conveniently forgot about during the investigation and hearing, he had received the reprimand and been relieved of command. What made the action even harder to take was that he was in line to receive a promotion and command of his own regiment. Under the circumstance, most men would have resigned and returned to a civilian life. Not Major Hodge. Just for spite, he remained in uniform, and a series of meaningless assignments followed. He knew his posting as the Troop Commander of the 98th Hospital was just another slap in the face and would be his last duty assignment. He was determined to make the most of it, and to make all those around him just as miserable as he was.

To say that Frank was shocked that night when he saw Colonel Hodge sitting in The Four Daughters laughing and talking over a beer with Hans Müller would be like saying that Moby Dick was just another fish. However, what Frank and the rest of the 98th Hospital didn't know was how much Hodge enjoyed sharing a beer and war stories with Hans. It was the only thing that made this assignment bearable for him. Both Hans and Hodge had been at Bastogne, and both had bittersweet memories from the battle. Colonel Hess who headed up the German attack had been to the Panzers what Patton was to the 3rd Army. The men that fought under them either worshiped them or hated their guts. Hess had been like a God to Hans. He worshiped him. The American Army had killed his hero at Bastogne, and he would never forgive them for that. Major Hodge's dreams of becoming a regimental tank commander had been shattered when he misread that order. Now both men, old and broken, with only their memories left would often get together to refight old battles over a few beers.

When Colonel Hodge received the final report on the Sergeant Lyons case he sent for Major Stovall. The longer he waited for Stovall to show up the more agitated he became. When Stovall walked into his office and saluted he exploded.

"What the hell is going on?" he yelled.

"Why don't you calm down and tell me what you are talking about?" Stovall said. However, Stovall already had enough experience in dealing with Hodge to know when he was in one of these moods it was impossible to have a rational conversation with him.

"This Lyons mess," Hodge said, waving the report he had received in Stovalls face.

"What about it?" Stovall said although he now knew why Hodge was so upset.

"Why is he being treated like some hero instead of the traitor he is?"

"What do you want me to do about it?"

"I want you to reopen this case and court martial him."

"Are you sure that is what you want?"

"Yes!"

"OK," Stovall said. "But let me explain what all that will involve. You will be called as a material witness and when on the stand you are going to have to explain all the information that's been leaking out of this office."

"What do you mean?"

"I mean that we have over a hundred documents that came through this office that were sent almost verbatim to the East Germans."

"Are you accusing me?" Hodge exploded.

"I'm accusing this office, and since you are the man in charge, well, yes I guess I'm accusing you."

"Do you realize what you are saying?"

"I most certainly do. Do you realize what will happen to you when I make these documents public?"

"You can't do that."

"I can, and I will if you insist on bringing Sergeant Lyons up on charges. There is a lot more going on that you apparently know nothing about, not only in your hospital, but in the region as well. Not to mention right here in your own office. Now are you going to shut up and sit down or do I bring charges against you?"

Stovall knew he shouldn't have spoken to the colonel that way, but he had wanted to tell Hodge to shut up ever since he had been assigned here. When he saw the look on Hodge's face he thought he might have gone too far. The Colonel sat back in his chair with a look of total defeat on his face. Stovall wanted to tell him about the CID agents he had been so concerned with, but knew that would be just too much information for the colonel to absorb right now.

"I take that as a yes," he said.

"Get the hell out of my office and out of my sight," Hodge said.

"Yes Sir!", and then Stovall came to attention, saluted, gave a smart military about face and walked out. Hodge didn't see the smile of satisfaction on his face. As he went by Sergeant Preston's desk he turned and told him they were going to need a new secretary. He then went in Helga's office and placed her under arrest.

"How long has he been in there?" Alexi asked as he walked into the office.

"Over an hour now," Andre replied. "He came in and asked for all the records we had in the Neubrücke file." Sergei was upset and someone was going to pay. When he heard about Uri he couldn't wait to get to the Stasi office in Trier to find out what was going on. The Trier office was headquarters for the Stasi directorate in this southwest corner of Germany and Alexi and Andre were the KGB liaison officers. Alexi knew they were in trouble when he saw Sergei looking at the records.

"Is there something in particular you are looking for?" he asked.

"Yes," Sergei answered. "I'm looking to see if there was ever any mention of our Birkenfeld operation in these reports."

"How could there be? No one over there knew about that."

"You better hope that's the case after the way you botched how Uri was taken care of. I couldn't believe it when I heard that idiot had killed that driver. No one was supposed to know we were involved in anything going on around here."

"We had nothing to do with that. We were just as surprised as you. Killing that man was entirely Uri's idea."

"Whose idea was it to kill Uri and leave his body for the Amis to find?"

"That was a mistake. He was supposed to die long before he did. We didn't get a chance to get rid of his body. Apparently he wasn't given enough poison."

"Obviously," Sergei said. Alexi though this was as good a time as any to give Sergei the other bad news.

"The woman has also been arrested," he said.

"Helga?" Sergei asked.

"Yes, do we need to take of her?"

"No. She doesn't know anything about our operation. The only part she played was selling information to the Stasi. Killing her would only draw more attention that we don't need right now. Uri is the one I'm worried about."

"But he won't be giving them any information."

"Don't be so sure about that. It won't take them long to find out who he was and maybe even that he was working for us. This whole operation may have just been exposed. My instincts are also telling me that someone else is now involved in what is going on around here. Those three agents at the hospital are not the only ones involved."

"Do we need to move in earlier than planned?"

"No. The equipment hasn't arrived. We need to be patient and learn as much as we can about what they are doing. We need that information and I will hang around as long as possible in order to get it. I'll be safe. They have been trying to catch me for a long time now, and haven't been successful. After I get the information I may even leave them something so they will know that Houdini was here."

TWELVE

BIRKENFELD TACTICAL AIR BASE

Just as Jeff, Claude and Frank were getting ready to enjoy a quiet evening in Höhns, Major Stovall walked in. "Mind if I join you," he said as he pulled up a chair and sat down.

"I got the information back on your driver, Jeff. We sent his finger prints to Washington and got some interesting info back. His name was Uri Stefaslaf. He was the son of a Russian diplomat and grew up in DC during the war. He returned to Russia along with his parents after the war. There's nothing more on him in any of our records until he showed up dead that morning. Washington thinks he was working for the KGB. Not as an agent, just working for them. Don't ask me why they think that, but they also think he was probably sent here to keep an eye on you. Now for the interesting part. The bar tender at the O Club is Horst Wagener. He is an East German Stasi informant. He has been working at the O Club for over three years and was there just to look and listen. Those folks have been placing agents and informants in various jobs at as many US bases over here as they can. They are doing all sorts of jobs like mechanics, drivers, secretaries, bar tenders, anywhere they can get in. Their main job is to listen to conversations and report anything interesting to the East Germans. So far as we have been able to find out the only thing Horst ever sent back to them in over three years was that three doctors and two nurses were being sent to the 24th Infantry Division for deployment to Lebanon. You caught Uri by surprise that afternoon when you ask him how to get in contact with him when you needed him again. He wasn't expecting that and didn't know what arrangements had been made for you to contact Joe. Telling the bar tender was the first thing he thought of. After you went in the club, he got word to Horst that he needed to talk to him. He explained what had happened and that you would be telling him when you needed to get in touch with him. They knew that each of them was working for the East Germans, but that was all they knew about each other. Horst did tell us that killing Joe was entirely Uri's idea. He had not been ordered to do that, and that was what got him killed. They didn't want us questioning him. So far as we've been able to determine neither of them knew anything about what was going on with Lyons."

"How did you get all of that information?" Jeff asked. "You didn't get all of that just from fingerprints."

"No, we didn't. Most of it we got from questioning Horst, other workers at the O Club, and various others around the hospital."

"How?" – But, before Jeff could go on Stovall interrupted him and said, "You'd be surprised what you can learn just from observation, and exercising a little influence as the chief of police. Being the Provost Marshal does have its advantages sometimes."

"What happens to Horst now?" Jeff asked.

"He gets a free trip back to the East as part of his plea bargain. However, I don't think it will be much of a bargain for him if they learn that he talked. I hear those people can be mean spirited over things like that. It wouldn't have been much better in one of the German prisons though. Some of the Germans tend to be sort of narrow minded where traitors are concerned."

"What about Helga?" Jeff asked. "Was there any connection between her and either of them?"

"Interesting question, and according to what Horst and others told us about that, she was not connected to any of this. Apparently, she was acting entirely alone. It's not even clear if she knew anything about Lyons. My best guess is that she set out to get her revenge and the Stasi found out what she was doing and tried to recruit her. According to a friend who wants to remain anonymous, she told them, and I quote, 'to go to hell.' According to this friend she didn't think any more of the Stasi than she did Americans. I have an idea though that her conversation with them is what gave her the notion of stealing information. It's only speculation, but she probably thought that if they were interested enough to ask her to spy, they might be willing to pay her for the information. We'll probably never know where or how she got that information to them, but she has one hell of a bank account. She was either the highest paid whore in Germany, or was being paid well for passing information on to the Stasi. My guess is she was a little of both"

"What happens to her now?"

"She'll probably be placed in a secure hospital facility so she can be treated for her problem. As you know she is in jail over in Baumholder. If one of the men she infected over there gets wind of what is going on she may not live long enough to go to trial. She is under watch in jail, but sometimes things get out of hand in spite of all we can do."

"You sound as if you wouldn't care if something did happen to her."

"The men that went to her in that whore house probably got what they deserved. But the innocent women they will infect back in the states don't deserve it. One of them could be someone in my family or a close friend. No, I guess I wouldn't care if Helga didn't live long enough to get out of that jail. I wouldn't even prosecute the man that killed her if I had that choice."

"Hey, sorry I butted in here," Stovall said. "Looks like you three were getting ready to celebrate."

"Celebrate?" Jeff asked.

"Yeah, you know, celebrate your victories. Getting your folks all out of East Germany in one piece and finding out who was sending information about the hospital to the Stasi. What happens now?"

"We don't know," Frank said.

"That's kind of what this is all about tonight," Claude said. "Trying to figure out where we go from here?"

"Good luck with that," Stovall said. "I just stopped by to give you the news about Uri and Horst. Let me know if I can help you in any other way." And, he got up and left.

"Where do we go from here?" Frank asked.

"I guess we figure out how we go about sticking our noses into the Birkenfeld Tactical Air Squadron's business?" Jeff said.

"No we don't," Claude replied. "What we do is start spending a lot of time in the gasthauses in and around Birkenfeld and keep our eyes and ears open. It might be a good idea to also start spending some time in their EM Club. I hear it is a little better than ours. It has slot machines and serves some of the best pizza in Germany."

"How do we get in?" Jeff asked.

"With our club cards. They honor our club cards just like our club honors theirs."

The military facility known as the Birkenfeld Air Base was first established by the German Wehrmacht as an anti-aircraft artillery battery in 1938. German Army soldiers of the 4th Anti-Aircraft Battery arrived in Birkenfeld during June of that year. In 1939, the unit was redesignated the 5th Battery as part of the 32nd Anti-Aircraft Regiment. There is an unconfirmed rumor that the base also served as a German hospital before the end of the war. The base facility is located on the outskirts of the town, and because of its location in the French Zone it was garrisoned by French troops after the war. The base and several tech site locations were turned over to the advance elements of the American 602nd Tac Con Sq during the summer and fall of 1948. These were the first American troops deployed to the French Occupation Zone.

The 602nd was soon welcomed to Birkenfeld with open arms when the townspeople learned they had come to build. Like all of Germany, Birkenfeld and the surrounding areas still faced a war-torn economy and were desperate for work. The Americans hired the local Germans and paid them well, and also paid the local business for what was needed to build Birkenfeld Air Base. Unlike the French who not only had not preformed even basic maintenance to the existing facilities, but had stripped the surrounding forests of millions of board feet of German timber and shipped it to France as well.

With their call sign of 'Cornbeef' the 602nd's primary mission was to provide early warning radar coverage and navigational aid to all aircraft flying over the occupied zones. They constructed and operated a Net Control Station or Master DF Site. This included a search radar, a height finder, several radio relay and direction finding sites and a high altitude traffic control center for all aircraft operating in occupied West Germany. In 1955, the 619th Tactical Control Squadron was moved to Birkenfeld. Their mission was to provide IFR (Instrument Flight Rules) control for all military and civilian aircraft flying above twenty thousand feet in West Germany. In addition, the squadron also established and operated several radio relay and direction finding sites. After getting all the military equipment installed and operational they set up a MARS station which permitted telephone calls to be patched back to the states to sweethearts, families and friends.

One of the first buildings constructed after all the military sites had been completed was an EM Club. The air force recognized the need to insure that troop morale remained high during the cold war years. This was especially important when bases were established in remote areas like Birkenfeld. Team sports were also given a high priority at the 602nd and they soon gained a reputation as a giant on the playing fields of Western Germany. The Taconeers, as they were known, finished third in the European Conference in 1956 and then won the USAFE Football Championship in 1957. The Birkenfeld Airmens Club became the scene of a wild and rowdy celebration.

In 1958, the 7424th Support Squadron took over all operations at what was now known as the Birkenfeld Tactical Air Base. They immediately began remodeling and restructuring the communications facilities to accommodate the growing number of jet aircraft operating in the skies over Europe. At least that's what the surrounding community and the world was told. What they were actually installing was a new, top secret communications system. Master Sergeant Tom Rogers was brought in to oversee the new construction and installation. Tom had helped design the new system and was one of only a handful of men qualified and had the necessary security clearance to operate the new equipment.

Tom Rogers had grown up on the outskirts of Cajun society in a little village just outside of Slidell, Louisiana. Not actually a Cajun, but wishing he was. He loved the outdoors and spent more time on the water and in the bayous of Cajun country chasing bass, catfish, crawdads and alligators than he did in school. By the time he entered high school this handsome country boy had already earned a reputation as a rebel. He learned at an early age that he didn't have to study to earn a passing grade. Some say he could have been one of the top students in his class. However, Tom would rather catch a bass or grovel for catfish than study for a math or English exam, and just earning enough points to graduate from school was all he cared about. He felt he never had to prove himself to anyone. He was who he was and that was all he ever tried to be. However, all that changed when only a month out of high school he joined the air force. He discovered radio communication and radar. After basic training at Barksdale Air Base he entered advanced training in communication and graduated at the top of his class.

Tom was especially excited about the new emerging computer technology. He recognized its potential in communications, and before graduating had already started designing computer enhanced communication stations. He envisioned someday when computers would operate air force radio and radar sites with speeds and efficiency that were unimaginable by the standards that were in place at the time. He was bound for a big letdown. His first duty assignment was as a repairman and troubleshooter to a remote radar tracking site in Turkey. His disappointment lasted only a few weeks though, when he realized the long boring hours waiting for an equipment breakdown could be used to work on his computer ideas. How to get his ideas recognized and accepted by the brass became his next project. He began by inserting drawings and sketches in every packet that went out from the site to the pentagon.

It took almost a year before someone recognized what they had and started trying to find where they came from. It took several more months before they traced the origin of the sketches and drawings to the mountain top in Turkey where Corporal Tom Rogers was and had him brought back to the states. Even then, it took another month of endless meetings and miles of red tape before anyone began to take Corporal Rogers seriously. Finally, a general who was tired of listening to conversations he couldn't understand and had no earthly idea of what Rogers was talking about said, "Enough. Young man, give me a set of working plans and specifications. I'll have some experts here look them over, and if they say it will work, we'll give it a try." That was all Tom wanted to hear. Six weeks later he had the information the general wanted and six months later, Sergeant Tom Rogers had the necessary backing and funds to build a working communications station.

The three men had made several trips to the airmans club in Birkenfeld and the Edelweiss Gasthaus without seeing Tom.

"Are you sure you will recognize him?" Claude asked after another fruitless trip. "I'm beginning to believe you only dreamed you met some man over here."

"I'm sure," Frank said. A few nights later Claude, Frank and Jeff were sitting in the airmans club in Birkenfeld eating pizza and feeding Marks to the slot machines when Tom walked in. Frank watched as the wheels of the slot machine stopped turning with three bunches of cherries showing. He dropped another Mark in the slot to get rid of the winner and scooped a handful of Marks from the tray and walked back over to the table where Claude and Jeff were sitting.

"That's him, that's Tom Rogers," he said as he was sitting back down.

After Tom had sat down, Frank got up and went over to his table and introduced himself and asked if Tom remembered him.

"Sure I do," he said.

"How about joining us? I'm with a couple of friends I'd like for you to meet." When they got back over to the other table, Frank said, "This is Tom Rogers, Tom this is Claude Morelocke and Jeff McReynolds."

After Tom was seated Frank said, "Claude is the post supply sergeant, and Jeff is a state department spy. He was sent over here by some senator trying to get reelected. He's supposed to be checking on how well our hospital operates."

"I think that's what they call a fact finding trip," Tom said.

"I feel at a disadvantage," Claude said.

"Why?" Tom asked.

"Well, I have to listen to an East Tennessee twang when these two are talking, and now I detect a distinct southern drawl when you talk. I feel out numbered."

"God talks the way we do," Tom said.

"Do I detect some Southern Louisiana in that?" Claude asked.

"Yep, Jambalaya, Crawfish Pie, Felé Gumbo and all that good stuff."

"I always thought that crawdads were fish bait," Frank said.

"That too. But, when they are boiled up with some big ears of sweet yellow corn and little red potatoes, yum-yum."

"You don't find much of that over here, do you?" Claude said.

"No, but sometimes a grilled bratwurst on a brötchen, smothered with sauerkraut and horse radish mustard while listening to Bobby Helms sing Fraulein helps fill the gap until I can get back home for some good chow."

After they got all the information about who talked funny and the food issues out of the way, the men began solving the worlds problems. Like why the Soviets beat the Americans into space with Sputnik and how if they had been in charge that would never have happened. After that, they started getting to know each other a little better by sharing what their jobs were, what they had done back home in civilian life, and how much longer their German tours were. Beer does have a way of making some folks long winded and telling things about themselves they wouldn't otherwise do.

"That was a very enjoyable evening," Claude said as they were driving back over to Neubrücke.

"Yes it was," Jeff said. "I like Tom. He seems very nice and knows a lot about what is going on at the air base."

"Maybe more than he told us. Why don't you have Harold find out a little more about him for us? We need to make sure he is not a spy or worse yet, a double agent before we get any more involved with him." It didn't take but a few days to get the information back on Tom. "He's the genuine article," Jeff told them a few evenings later. "According to my source in Washington, he is a communications expert, and was sent over here to oversee the upgrade to the new facility they are building here. But,--"

"Why do I have an uneasy feeling about that but," Frank said before Jeff could continue.

"This time there's a good reason for your feelings," Jeff continued. "There's also some doubt about Tom's legitimacy. He may be a double agent, or even a spy."

"How could they put someone like that in charge of such a secret project?" Claude asked.

"Good question, and, one to which there's no clear answer. It seems the air force had some serious questions about giving him the job after their investigation turned up the fact that he may be working for the other side. However, the FBI insisted that they go ahead with the project with Tom in charge."

"What's the FBI got to do with it?" Frank asked.

"That's the sixty four dollar question," Jeff said.

"An even bigger question is what are we going to do about it?" Claude said.

"Harold suggests we play along and see what happens, but to be careful. We don't want to spook him if something is going on," Jeff said.

"You three were not completely truthful with me the last time you were over here," Tom said as he slid into a seat with them at the Edelweiss Gasthaus.

"In what way?" Jeff asked.

"In just about every way. I did some checking, and it seems you three are not what you led me to believe. I found out that I'm dealing with a couple of CID men and a CIA detective. Would you like to start over again and explain what is going on?"

"We meant no disrespect," Jeff said. "But, I offer no apology either. I guess it's the nature of the games we play. We all have our little secrets."

"What's that supposed to mean?" Tom asked.

"It seems you weren't completely honest with us either. We did some checking also, and it turns out you know a lot more about what is going on around here than you let on."

"Oops," Tom said. "I guess we've gotten ourselves a Mexican standoff. What happens now?"

"I hope it wasn't caused by those jumping beans," Frank said.

"Now that we have that out of the way do you want to start all over again?" Jeff asked.

"Why not." Tom said.

"I don't know how much you know about us, but just to clear the air," Jeff said. "We were sent over here because of something that was going on at the hospital. Someone was sending information about the hospital to the East Germans and it had our agencies worried. What we were sent to look into turned out to be nothing. Most of the stuff that was being sent over there was nothing more than garbage and was probably a diversion. We think someone was trying to keep us busy looking elsewhere while the bad guys were involved in something more important. Maybe right under our noses. Right now we don't know what is really going on, but it certainly wasn't what we were sent over here for. We did get involved in a couple of interesting side tracks while working on that case, but we do wonder what they are trying to keep us from finding. However, it seems there are some intriguing rumors floating around about your air base."

"They're not rumors," Tom said.

"What?" Claude said.

"The fact that we are doing a lot of remodeling and construction is well known. What is not so widely known is that most of the construction that is going on is for the installation of a state of the art computer enhanced communications facility."

"That was quite a mouth full," Frank said. "And, I haven't the slightest idea what you're talking about."

"What we're putting in here is a communications and air control center that will be decades ahead of anything the Soviets, or the rest of the world for that matter, have the capability for. The Soviets in particular will do anything to get their hands on what we have here. They have already tried."

"What do you mean?" Claude asked.

"We caught a couple of the construction workers trying to get out the gate with a set of plans."

"If this place is so important why don't you have better security?" Jeff asked.

"We have good security. It's just not visible. We wanted to keep it low key so as not to draw too much attention to what was going on. Besides, we haven't started on the installation of equipment and getting it operational. That will be when the real secret stuff starts. The folks that will be working on that have to pass a security clearance I'm not sure I could pass."

"Is there anything we can do to help?" Jeff asked.

"Sure. Anytime you're over this way keep your eyes and ears open. After that caper you just pulled over at the hospital every agent around here will know who you are. If they see you all nosing around here it could cause them to get even more curious about what we are doing, and we don't need that. But, I appreciate the offer."

"We understand," Frank said.

"Tell you what," Tom said. "If and when things start popping I'm sure we could use some more boots on the ground then. When we need help, I'll send for the cavalry, OK?"

"Good enough," Jeff said.

"Do you feel like we've just been told to piss off?" Claude asked as they were driving back to the hospital.

"Yes," Jeff said. "But, after all we have no business, and no authority over there, and we were butting in without orders."

"What do we do now?" Frank asked.

"I guess we go home and go to bed," Claude said.

"You know that's not what I mean."

"I know, but it's a good idea," Jeff said. "That's about all we can do for now. I'll talk to Harold in the morning and see what he suggests."

"You can't do anything more right now," Harold told Jeff when he was told what had happened at Birkenfeld yesterday. "I've asked Langley for help, but haven't heard back from them yet. As for your army buddies, it's an inner service matter now. They can't do anymore unless the air force invites the army in, and that's not likely to happen. Like I told you before, you all accomplished what you were sent over here to do. It's time now to walk away and let someone else do their jobs."

"What happens next for me?" Jeff asked.

"Relax and enjoy a little down time. Go to the worlds fair. You may never get another chance to visit one on the government's money. I'm sure the company will have another assignment for you in the near future."

"What's going on Tom?" Claude asked as they came through the door.

"I told you all I would let you know if and when anything happened. When I came in this morning I found this mess."

"Any idea what they were looking for?"

"Yes. The communications tapes."

"The what?"

"The computer tapes. It's the magnetic tape that contains the instructions to make all this stuff operate. Without those tape all this equipment is useless. It's just another pile of junk."

"Are the tapes gone?"

"Yes, along with the plans."

"What plans?"

"The construction plans."

"Any idea who's responsible?" Frank asked.

"Oh yes," Tom said and then he started laughing.

"Someone breaks into your office, steals secret tapes and plans, and you can laugh about it. I don't understand?"

"I might be able to shed some light on that." Major Stovall said as he came through the door.

"Do you know what's going on Frank?" Claude asked.

"I haven't the foggiest notion, but I think we've just been had," Frank said.

"Not at all boys," Stovall said. "Have a seat and I'll explain. And, by the way, it's Alan Crandall, FBI, and not Major Stovall." The three men couldn't believe what they had just heard.

"Three, maybe four years ago when this place was just a dream, someone at the pentagon began to have doubts about building such an important and secret facility as this way out here in the boon docks with no security," Alan explained. "It originally was supposed to have been built in Frankfurt at Rhine-Maine, but the air force nixed that idea. They wanted it entirely away from any existing air ports, especially one as large and busy as Rhine-Maine. They felt too much security would draw too much attention and they didn't want that. They also said that all the communication that is required for normal airport operations would interfere with what they were going to build. The argument went on for several months. Then several factors fell into place that allowed the construction to start. Tom was the daddy of the whole thing and had built a working prototype of what he wanted this facility to look like. He just didn't know at the time where it would be built. While all that was going on Colonel Hodge started hollering about having an MP detachment stationed at the 98th hospital. He was told the MP's at Baumholder could provide all he needed. He wasn't satisfied with that arrangement and started calling in some IOU's. He wanted to feel like a real base commander and wanted the hospital treated just like a large military base. The 7th Army brass gave in and the colonel got his MP's. Meanwhile, back in Washington the FBI had been tracking a Russian KGB agent. We knew they had managed to infiltrate the lower echelons of the CIA offices. We also managed to get a double agent involved and just before moving in to take down the Russian operative, he and the FBI agent turned up dead. The police found them floating in the Potomac, and the KGB agent they had been following fled the country. We didn't know how much damage had been done, and before we could assess what had happened, that agent turned up here in Birkenfeld. It was assumed he had somehow found out about what was planned for the air base here, and I was sent over to keep an eye on him. However, we didn't want him to know that we were onto to him or that the FBI was involved. Since the MP detachment had just been formed at the 98th I was given a cover as the Provost Marshal of Colonel Hodges MP's."

"But, how could the FBI be involved?" Claude asked.

"Good question. And, there were two reasons. First, the bad guys wouldn't expect it, and technically in a matter of speaking, American bases are American soil so the FBI could get involved."

"That's really stretching the truth." Jeff said.

"Maybe," Alan said. "But when did Hoover ever let a little truth get in his way? Also, in case you are wondering, I am a qualified MP. After graduating from the MP school at Fort Gordon in 1942 I was sent to England. I was there for all the buildup prior to the invasion and was in one of the units responsible for the security surrounding all that. After the invasion, I followed Patton's 3rd Army across France and Germany. I was a platoon sergeant when the war ended. When I got back home I found out the FBI was looking for a few good ex-military men. Then, two years ago when this thing was being planned I got the job because of my military background. That's how I wound up as the Provost Marshal of Colonel Hodges new MP detachment."

"Now I'm beginning to understand," Jeff said. "Being FBI is how you got all that information you gave us several days ago. I never did believe that story about how being the Provost Marshal opens doors baloney you fed us."

"I still don't understand," Frank said.

"That was the beauty of the plan," Alan said. "No one would suspect an MP at that hospital to be part of the security at the air base. The real fun started when those reports from the hospital started showing up in the East German Stasi's hands. That caught us by surprise. We were still trying to figure out what was going on and what to do about it when the CID got involved. I didn't think much of their capabilities after watching them botch some investigations during the war. Then when you two clowns showed up it only solidified my feelings. However, you have restored my faith in our intelligence capabilities. You are good, almost as good as the FBI."

"Only almost?" Claude asked.

"Almost," Alan said.

"OK," Frank said. "What about the tapes and plans?"

"Oh, don't worry about those," Tom said. "All the Germans got was some good ole oompah band music and plans to a drive in restaurant."

"I don't understand?"

"The tapes they took were nothing more than some band music and the plans were for a good ole American drive-in."

"That was Tom's idea," Alan said. "When we found out the KGB might be involved Tom cooked up the idea with the fake tapes and plans."

"I started leaving the plans lying around whenever I would go out and occasionally at night," Tom said. "The real plans are in a safe up at the bunker. I made a big to-do about the tapes arriving and brought a couple of tapes in to work with me yesterday morning. I also had some crates brought in and told everyone the equipment had arrived and we would start installing it today. The real equipment arrived over a week ago and is in Alan's office with the MP's guarding it. The real tapes haven't even arrived yet."

"You mean all this is fake?" Frank asked.

"Every bit of it," Tom said. "However, there is one other little surprise in those tapes. There is a bug in them."

"What do you mean – bug?"

"It's a computer program that will mess up their computers so bad they will be useless for a long time. We hope they don't catch on that the tape is what is making their computers sick and will try it in every one they have. If they do, they will be playing catch up for a long-long time."

"I didn't understand a word you just said."

"Don't worry. Most people don't. Just trust me. I couldn't help but laugh a while ago when I thought of them when they put those tapes in their machines and all they hear is that band music. Can't you just see them if they try to use those plans and instead of a communications station they wind up with a drive-in hamburger joint."

And, they all laughed.

"But what about Tom?" Jeff asked. "When we ran a background check on him before getting involved here the report came back that he might be a double agent."

"That came about because he was working with the FBI to set this thing up. Neither the air force nor any of the other agencies were told about that. When the air force did their security check before giving the go ahead for this project that little bit of information showed up on him. The FBI had to do some quick shuffling around to convince the air force to go ahead with Tom as the head of this project."

"What about those agents the DC police pulled out of the Potomac?" Frank asked. "When we told you about that before you acted like you didn't know anything about it."

"More of the game," Alan said. "Like I just told you, there was also a KGB agent associated with them and we didn't know how much you might have known about that. Some more of that if you don't know, I'm not going to tell you stuff that was going on at the time."

"You mean all this has just been a scam?" Claude asked.

"I'm not sure scam is the right word," Alan said. "But, yes it was all designed to fool the bad guys."

"Frank, I told you we were just being used," Claude said.

"Several times," Frank said.

"Don't feel so bad boys," Jeff said. "Looks like we've all been had."

"None of you should feel bad," Alan said. "You all played your parts to perfection. Even better than expected. And, now let me tell you the rest story."

"After that Sputnik thing went up all the American intelligence agencies were scrambling around trying to explain how it could have happened. Truth is they were all caught with their pants down. While they were still trying to figure out what happened, CIA agents in East Germany started intercepting those reports about an American military hospital. After discovering where the hospital was the pentagon was shaking its head and asking why. Almost everyone knew the reports coming out of the 98th Hospital were meaningless. However, they couldn't just be ignored. Especially when a project such as the one being planned for the air base here was in the same area. Because of that the Department of Defense grounded the air force plans until someone figured out what was going on at the hospital. The whole project was put on hold for six months. That gave Tom a chance to attend the Air Force Security Forces Academy at Lackland Air Force Base in Texas so he could become an Air Police Security Agent. In addition to being a computer geek, he is also one heck of a security agent."

"That's what he meant the other day when he said they had good security here," Claude said.

"Yeah, between some specially trained Air Police, Tom and myself, I'd say the Birkenfeld Air Base has about the best security of any military installation around here. While at the academy, Tom got the idea to let the East Germans think we had taken the bait and play along with them. That way we could find out what was really involved. But, we couldn't have real agents snooping around. They would see in a minute what was going on."

"So, why not send in a couple of dummies like us?" Frank said.

"That's not exactly the way I would put it," Alan said. "But yes, we needed someone without a lot of experience, however at the same time we had to have someone the East Germans could believe in. Anyway, the plan almost didn't get off the ground when Major Bradley got involved. Somehow Bradley found out what was going on and insisted that he should be the one to run the show. I think it would have been an entirely different outcome if Stevens hadn't decided to stop in at The Four Daughters before reporting for duty. I'm sure glad we never had to find out. I think you could hear Hoover and the FBI boys in DC applauding all the way over here when you put Bradley down like you did Jess – do you mind if I call you Jess?"

"Not at all – in fact I think I prefer it."

"Jess?" Frank asked.

"Jess Millsap, and I grew up just across the mountain from you in Roan Mountain."

"Well I'll be damned," Frank said.

"Can I get back to my story?" Alan asked.

"No one was supposed to know about my involvement, and apparently no one did because the next thing I knew Harold was snooping around," Alan said.

"And, that's how I got involved," Jess said.

"I guess so. Apparently Harold brought you in not only to find out what was going on, but to keep an eye on the CID as well. However, you three about ruined it for everyone. When you two figured out what was going on and the thing about Lyons' wife came out it caught us all by surprise. You weren't supposed to be so capable, and that thing about Lyons' wife really threw a monkey wrench into the works. That wasn't supposed to be part of the game. It took some real scrambling around and head scratching to let you send that green agent into East Germany. However, Harold decided that since Bobby Joe was one of his best agents he could take care of Irma. Another surprise we got was when Helga got involved. No one had even noticed the stuff she was sending over the border until you figured it out Frank. If Jess hadn't gotten involved with her we might not have ever figured that one out. Even though you didn't know you were part of the script, you guys played your part to perfection. You kept the KGB and Stasi agents believing that all we were interested in was catching a spy at the hospital. That allowed Tom to put his plan into action over here, and as the man once said, the rest is history."

"Was Harold involved in all this?" Jess asked.

"If you mean, did he know what was going on, no, not until the very last. That's what I meant when I said he started snooping around. He had not been told of my involvement, but started getting suspicious when you all figured out the Lyons thing was only a diversion. As you know our agencies don't like to share what they know with each other, or work very well together. Professional jealousy I think you call it. That business with what happened to you in Puerto Rico didn't help matters any either. As for what Harold knew, and when he knew it, you will have to ask him about that.

"Not so fast," Frank said. "There are still a lot of unanswered questions here."

"Yeah," Claude said. "Back there when we were investigating Joe's murder you acted like we were a surprise to you."

"All part of the act," Alan said. "I knew there was a CID agent at the hospital. What I didn't know was who it was or that there were two of you. I also didn't know about Jess until he was questioning Lyons and told Bradley who he was."

"Yeah," Jess said. "That was a slip of the tongue. I was so pissed at Bradley I didn't know what I was saying. After it was all over I didn't know whether to say anything more or not. I decided to play it dumb and let you make the next move."

"I couldn't believe what I had heard. I knew you had slipped and decided to let it go. Each of us was let in on only what we needed to know at the time. That's what made it all so believable. If I had known who or what you were Claude, when you pulled that crystals for my radios business I would have skinned you alive. That wasn't part of the act. I needed those radios. You two surprised us all. We never planned on you being as capable as you are. You almost ruined it for us. You kept us scrambling to stay ahead of you. I actually thought you were just a couple of bumbling beer guzzling womanizers. When Jess told me that afternoon that you were CID I couldn't believe it. How could I with the reputation you had. Then I started watching you. I've never seen anyone who could act drunker after sucking on one bottle of beer all night. As for the women, I don't know how you managed to spread that rumor. But, that's all it was, just a lot of bragging and talk."

"Guilty as charged," Frank said. "All designed to pick up as much gossip as we could. It was all Claude's idea. He came up with the plan after that first night we were out. It wasn't hard to act dumb, at least not for me, and it has been a lot of fun. We did hear some good stories, especially about ourselves. I wish we could have done some of the things we've been accused of."

"You two ought to consider acting as a career after your military obligations are over," Alan said.

"Back to business," Tom said. "Did our plan work?"

"Not like we planned, but good enough I think," Alan said. "The two that broke into your office were two of the construction workers. Apparently they had been paid by either the KGB or Stasi for their efforts. The AP's had no trouble following them and watching them turn over the booty to the real agents. However, they lost those agents trail, and when we went to arrest the KGB agent he was gone also. We have an alert out for them, but the chances of finding them now are slim and none. They probably hightailed it for Trier where they are being hidden in one of the many espionage groups there. It looks like we gave the cheese to the mice and let them get away with it."

"That KGB man was Houdini," Alan continued. "Sometimes he leaves something to let us know that it was him. This time he left a note thanking us for the information. We know he was in Washington and escaped before we could catch him. That's the reason for the name. He's an escape artist. He has escaped from Britain's MI6 Units and us so many times he's become a legend. My guess is that's what he was doing in Washington, and when he found out what the air force was planning he came over here to find out what was going on. As I said before, we knew he was snooping around in Washington. He's probably the one that set up that diversion at the hospital so no one would notice him in Birkenfeld. That diversion gave him plenty of time to set everything up over here. It's hard telling how many more agents he recruited that are still watching what's going on around here. Sergei is one of the Kremlin's best agents. He is one of the most wanted in both England and the US because of his espionage capabilities. Sometimes he comes in on an opt – gets the info he needs – and is gone before we realize he's there. Other times he comes in and we know he is in the area, but before we can capture him he slips through our fingers. That's why both us and the British have nicknamed him Houdini. There have been times when both of us have had him cornered and when we moved in there was no one there. He's a master of disguise and is almost ghostlike. He also likes to taunt us. That's why he usually leaves a calling card."

"I guess it's not so bad to have been beaten by the best," Claude said.

"Maybe not," Alan said. "But, it sure hurts when it happens over and over again."

"It may not be all that bad this time," Tom said.

"How so?" Alan asked.

"Because, when he gives that tape to them and they try to use it in their computer it will mess it up so bad they won't be using the computer for a long-long time."

"You mentioned that once before," Claude said. "What are you talking about?"

"I put a program on that tape that messes up the computers logic. Don't try to understand. Just believe me. If they try to use that tape in their computer it will screw it up so bad it will be useless for a long time."

"What's so important about this new communications station here anyway?" Claude asked.

"It's not the station that's important," Tom said. "It's the computer technology that will be used in it that makes it important."

"You keep talking about computers, technology, computer bugs, and all that stuff," Claude said. "I thought all that was just science fiction."

"It's not science fiction anymore. It was a computer that helped launch Sputnik and kept it in orbit as long as it did. If they would have had just half the computer technology that will be in this station here, that thing would still be flying. Don't you remember how they used a computer to predict the outcome of the 1952 presidential election?"

"Yes, but that thing was as big as a house. How in the world could the Russians have one of those on that little Sputnik thing?"

"Transistors," Tom said.

"Transistors?"

"Yes, the same technology that makes your little transistor radio work. The first computers were built using vacuum tubes and because of that had to be as big as a house as you put it. However, with the invention of transistors they are much smaller now, and they didn't have one in Sputnik, they used computers to guide it into orbit. This new unit we are building here will be a combination communications and tracking station much like what is here now. However, it will have enhanced computer technology built into it. That's what's in those crates in Alan's office. Computers. Computers that will make this station decades ahead of anything anywhere in the world. This will be a test facility. It will be used to prove that the technology will work and to get the bugs out of it. If it proves out here like I think it will, the air force will build stations like this one at several locations around the world. The Russians are way behind us in communications computer technology, and if that bug I put in the tape their agent stole works out like I planned, they will be even farther behind. They will do anything they have to in order to get their hands on what we know. That's why those men were sent here, and it won't be the last time they try to get their hands on what we know.

Some day computers will revolutionize the communications industry. Satellites with onboard computers will be circling the earth and will change forever the way we communicate. Tracking stations like the one we are building here will be in place all around the globe to monitor and communicate with them."

"You've been drinking some bad beer, and it's distorted your thinking," Claude said.

"If they can put those things in satellites I wonder if there will ever be a computer we can hold in our hand." Frank said.

"You've been drinking the same bad beer," Claude said.

"Speaking of drinking," Frank said. "Let's go up to the Edelweiss and get a beer. I hear they have a new waitress there that's really something."

"Now you're speaking a language I can understand," Claude said. "Who wants to go with us?" And they all piled into Claude's Plymouth.

"Computers!" Claude mumbled as he started the car and reached for the 'D' button on the dashboard console that controlled his push button drive transmission.

Epilogue

I n September of 1958, the 6th Convalescent Center was deactivated and the personnel stationed there assigned to the 98th Hospital. The 6th CC was reactivated as a fifteen hundred bed rehab hospital at Cam Rahn Bay, Viet Nam in early 1969. The cluster of buildings housing the reactivated 6th CC was built atop a sun splashed slope overlooking the South China Sea. An hour after midnight on 11 August of that year the hospital was attacked by Viet Cong Sappers that had cut their way through the barbed wire surrounding the hospital. Nineteen of the hospitals ninety four buildings were burned to the ground. Miraculously only two of the hospitals patients were killed in the attack. Ninety eight more were seriously injured. The hospital later came under political fire for being the army's most notorious amnesty drug compound in Viet Nam. Sometimes housing over two hundred junkies at a time.

The 98th General Hospital was deactivated in 1970, and the fifty five building complex turned over to the German government. It has at various times since then been used as a school and has housed Army, Air Force and NATO units. The site was eventually razed, and an American style university campus built where the old 98th and 6th CC Hospitals had once been.

The 7424th Support Sqdn not only continued base housekeeping and maintenance responsibilities at the Birkenfeld Air Base after they built the new communications center, but they also supported a growing list of tenant organizations that were assigned to the base. On July 1, 1962 control of Birkenfeld Air Base was passed to the 615th AC & W Squadron. The arrival of the 615th commenced a decade long buildup of the air station and related facilities. The Rhein Upper Area Control Center – previously Cornbeef Control was operated by both the US and German Air Forces there until 1968. Constant training of assigned personnel and NATO counterparts was the order of the day. The cost-cutting days of the Nixon years spelled the end for the once proud Birkenfeld Air Base. The air station was turned over to the German Army (Bundeswher) on December 31, 1969 and was renamed the Oldenburg Kaserne.

In an ironic twist of fate, when the Birkenfeld Air Base was shut down the troops stationed there were sent for a time five kilometers down the road to the run-down, mothballed hospital complex in Neubrücke that had once been home to the 98th General Hospital and 6th Convalescent Center.

When Fraulein sung by Bobby Helms debuted in 1957 it immediately went to number one on the country charts and remained there for four weeks. It remained a top ten hit for the next fifty two weeks. One couldn't walk into a gasthaus or club in Germany where there was a juke box during that time without hearing Bobby Helms sing Fraulein at least once. It's still the number one song for all of us who served in Germany during that time.

FRAULEIN - Lyrics and music written by Lawton Williams

Far across deep blue water, lives an old German's daughter,
by the banks of the old river Rhine.
Where I loved her and left her, but I can't forget her,
I miss my pretty Fraulein.

AFTERWORD

Jean's VW Bug parked behind the 6th CC
barracks in Neubrücke, Germany

After Jean got back home from Germany and settled down from
the scare about her Mom, she wrote me and said for me to buy a
Volkswagen (VW) Bug. At the time it didn't seem possible. Porsche had
just restarted production of their popular little VW Bug and the GI's
were buying them faster than they could produce them. There was a six
months waiting list for them in Germany, and I was only going to be
there another three to four months. One of the German secretaries in

the medical records office at the hospital heard that I was looking for a VW and told me her uncle in Saarbrucken had a VW dealership and she thought she could get me one. A few weeks later I was at the VW dealer in Saarbrucken watching them unload my new 1958 blue VW bug that I had paid $1192 for.

When it came time for me to come home the army shipped the VW home for me. Another of the perks that came with being an NCO. When I got the orders sending me home, I was disappointed to see that I would be making the trip back home on the same troop ship I had come to Germany on a little over a year ago. After my experience on that trip, I wasn't looking forward to this one. However, this trip on the USNS Upshur was much smoother, and I got into New York harbor at daylight on Friday, December 20th 1958, sailing right by The Statue of Liberty just as the sun was coming up. There was a rumor going around that we would have to stay on the ship all weekend because the dock workers didn't work on weekends. However, we were docked at Brooklyn Army Terminal shortly after noon and were soon off the ship and on our way to Fort Hamilton. Usually the army sent people being discharge to an army base as near to their home as possible. However, if you were picking up a car, you got discharged at Fort Hamilton.

By late Tuesday afternoon, December 23, I was beginning to think I might have to spend Christmas at Fort Hamilton. The army wasn't going to discharge me. After everyone else had been processed, Lt Callie Cook, who was in charge of the processing center, explained it to me this way. He said that I had only been on loan to the army for a couple of years, and since I had enlisted through my local National Guard unit I would have to be transferred back to them, not discharged. He said the order had already been cut and wished me a Merry Christmas. I got my orders transferring me from the US Army to the 330th AAA Battalion, Tennessee Army National Guard, Kingsport, Tennessee, and after driving all night got back to Tennessee on Christmas Eve. It was the first time Jean had seen her VW and the first time I had seen home in over a year.

A few days after Christmas we were out driving and got stopped by a highway patrol road block. We were in the VW, and it still had the army license plates from Germany on it, and the only drivers license I had was my German license. The patrolman looked at the drivers license, then at me, then back at the license, and then he walked around to the front of the car and looked at the license plate. He just shook his head, and while handing my license back he said, "You sure are a long way from home Freddie." No. I wasn't a long way from home. I was a long way from Neubrücke, and glad that adventure was over.

FA Shepherd

ACKNOWLEDGEMENTS

I would like to thank Carl for making my year with the 6th Convalescence Center bearable and for providing the foreword and pictures of the hospital complex for this book. Thanks also for your friendship over the years and for the computer help you have so generously provided.

I would also like to thank Geneva, one of the army wives that lived at Höhn's, for befriending Jean and making her time in Germany the fun trip that it was, and for providing the post card with the picture of Höhn's gasthause for this book.

Other Books by FA Shepherd

HORSE CREEK LEMONADE

In this fiction novella, Shepherd weaves a delightful tale of industrial espionage and conspiracy. Horse Creek Chemical Company is on the verge of bankruptcy due to the arrogance and incompetence of a former president. Chemicals from kudzu including a new biofuel that could free Horse Creek from dependence on foreign oil promises to ease the companies money problems, but an explosion and fire in their pilot plant may dash those hopes. When a former employee is brought back to investigate the accident he discovers drugs, terrorists and a moonshing operation that could cause Horse Creek much bigger problems than a fire in their pilot plant. The unorthodox methods he uses to deal with the drugs, terrorists, and a nosy revenuer causes even more problems. Horse Creek Lemonade deals with industrial problems as old as the chemical industry and as new as today's headlines about illegal immigrants, terrorists and drug problems.

THE MASSACRE AT NOE CREEK – A COLLECTION OF STORIES AND TALES

The Massacre at Noe Creek combines history, fiction and some of the author's own experiences to weave a set of tales that will delight and fascinate anyone who opens it. The title story of The Massacre at Noe Creek spans the time between the Civil War and some 15 years after the end of WW II. This story exemplifies Shepherd's ability to seamlessly blend history and fiction to create a riveting narrative. In the book's second story, Colonial Heights Road, Shepherd combines his own coming of age with the early history of this Kingsport bedroom community. With vivid detail, Shepherd describes life in this small crossroads community during the 1940's. The Massacre at Noe Creek is a collection of 15 partly truth and partly fiction stories and tales that skillfully transports readers to places and times forgotten and unknown with settings as exotic as Moscow and as mundane as the local fishing hole.

THE SECRETS OF HICKORY HOLLOW

The Secrets of Hickory Hollow revolves around the history of the lives of rugged Scottish pioneers that settle in an isolated southern Appalachian Mountain valley. Over the years their little settlement grows and establishes itself as an independent community complete with a church, a school, and government policies and laws of its own. During the mid to late 1940's in the aftermath of WW II the residents of Hickory Hollow are caught up in the changing times that lead their lives and the community into an intricate web of lies, deception, crimes and greed. A sheriff that dispenses justice with his heart instead of the law, a G Man with his own ideas about history and a Cherokee half breed have to cope with revenuers, Nazis, murder and some of the communities own prejudices in order to restore Hickory Hollow back to the peaceful and quiet little crossroads bedroom community it once was.

For more information about these books and about the author please visit oldshepbooks.com.

CPSIA information can be obtained at www.ICGtesting.com
Printed in the USA
LVOW050624110712

289547LV00003B/22/P